Running Away

*from or to
the Truth?*

Yvette Samaan
Author of Running Away, from or to God?

PUBLISH
AMERICA

PublishAmerica
Baltimore

First printing

✦

ISBN: 1-59129-896-2
PUBLISHED BY PUBLISHAMERICA BOOK
PUBLISHERS
www.publishamerica.com
Baltimore

Printed in the United States of America

This book is lovingly dedicated to

*My father **George**, who taught me that nothing was impossible.*
*My sister **Lily**, who believed in me.*
*My husband **Nader**, who was the wind beneath my wings.*
*My daughters **Gisele** and **Adora**, who taught me the real meaning of love.*

Table of Contents

Part Two
The Everlasting Cycle of Truth

INTRODUCTION

The twentieth century had witnessed the birth of many inventions and discoveries. As we entered the century, we were accompanied by light in our homes and streets. One might think that electric light had helped us see better. This can be partly true because this manmade light exposes whatever matter it is directed on, but it doesn't go beyond the materialistic and the mundane.

Even though electric light has shed light on "things," it did not help us improve our sense of sight. On the contrary, we might have developed a peculiar kind of blindness: Blindness of the heart.

Yes, we have the most cherished physical faculty, the ability to see with our physical eyes. And yes, we have manmade light plus God-made light. Nevertheless, the presence of these three amenities together doesn't necessarily produce the ability to see with our hearts.

There are two kinds of blindness of the heart that I will refer to as **selective blindness**, and **spiritual blindness**. Selective blindness allows us to shut out what we don't want to see. As if we pulled the shade on the window of our hearts so we wouldn't see the crucial needs of people, and even our own sins and guilt. Distressed people are all around us peering hungrily, waiting for us to satisfy their physical or spiritual hunger. We do have the food; yet, we don't bother sparing it lest our contact with these people should interfere with our enjoyment of our life. Perhaps the alluring bright light of the world has blinded us to the extent that we don't see people and their needs anymore. The sad part about having selective blindness is that we choose to draw the drapes and we surround our hearts with darkness for fear of looking outside and seeing our sins written in big scarlet letters.

The cause of selective blindness could be traced back to another kind of blindness: spiritual blindness. We are spiritually blind when we look the opposite direction from God and continue living in our sin. Of course we will be able to see plenty of "things," yet, nothing from the realm of God. In this sinful state, we may be looking for the truth, but going in the wrong direction, will not serve the purpose. Thus, we fail to see God and **His truth**. Disoriented, some people develop **pseudo-spirituality** as they focus solely on the **spirit of man** rather than the **Spirit of God**. They **believe in their own righteousness** rather than **the righteousness granted by a Savior** and live a **pseudo truth** focusing on the **creation of God** rather than on **God the Creator**.

Pseudo-spirituality was exemplified by the atrocious act of the terrorists on September 11, 2001. Focusing on themselves and on their own version of truth, they ran full speed towards a destination far, far away from God; thus, demonstrating their spiritual blindness and, in the process, many people were hurt.

The truth is that we fail to see God in our life because we do not have Him in our hearts. How could we when we are looking the other way, or running away from His truth? If we are to see God, we ought to be touched by Jesus Christ, our Savior and Healer, and become a new creation **in Him** and **He in us**. We have to be grafted into the olive tree (Jesus Christ) in order to be in Him and get the nourishment of life in us.

Running Away, from or to the Truth? depicts the above picture and presents it in two sections. The first part, presents vignettes of people in a vicious cycle aiming at avoiding the truth at all costs, and living in their selective and spiritual blindness. Turning their backs to God, they follow their manmade light – only to wake up and find themselves in the darkest night.

The second part portrays people in the everlasting cycle of truth, people who follow **the true light** of Jesus Christ. In Him they can see, not only with sound eyes, but also with their hearts and souls. Jesus Christ is their eye opener and the healer of their dim eyesight. Thus, they are able to see His truth.

I would like to invite you, the reader, to examine these characters I have portrayed. Then, let us learn together from their mistakes or right doings. May the exposure of their misconception lead us to the knowledge of truth! May the depiction of their sound faith in Christ inspire us to allow Him to open our eyes and lead us in His light!

Part One

Trapped
In Our
Imaginary Truth

"I am the way, and the truth, and the life; no one comes to the Father, but by Me."

(John 14:6)

Hush Up Your Conscience

"Whither shall I go from Thy Spirit?
Or whither shall I flee from Your presence?
If I ascend to heaven, Thou art there!"
(Psalms 139:7, 8)

Long time ago, the Ammonites used to give sacrifices to their god, Molech. To appease Molech, the parents had to offer their firstborn baby boy or girl as a sacrifice to him. The way they practiced that ritual was appalling, yet interesting. The priest would take the baby from his mother's arms and place him or her in Moleck's arms, and then start the fire. You can imagine the deafening, horrifying sound of the crying and wailing of both the baby and the parents. However, the solution to this was to beat the drums so the horrendous voices may disperse in the resonance of a louder sound.

It seems like human beings were working against themselves to satisfy an imaginary authority (the idol). Now, the question is: do we mimic the same script in the present time? Do we try to appease an imaginary authority (the world) at the expense of the truth?

Think of all the times we tried to hush up our conscience by justifying why we had to sin, for example. Think of how many times we went to corner bars or rowdy parties, engaged in very rambunctious activities, or told ourselves lies just to create a voice much louder than our conscience hoping that we could find a cure for our guilt. Here, we try to buy or drink our way out of guilt and misery – only to wake up the next day with the worst hang over ever.

We may succeed for a while, but God's voice is even louder than the tumult we want to bring along. His truth will eventually be revealed and enforced whether we like it or not. It's not that God wants to torture us, or give us the guilt trip. His desire is to put an end to the piercing noises of the drums and have the tender sound of His truth and love make a debut in our life.

Beat, Beat the Drums

My sins are before my eyes
Their voice is loud and clear.
I can even hear their cries
Almost deafening my ear.

They wake my guilty conscience
Telling me I am no good,
They came with a vengeance
To destroy my livelihood.

I try to leave my guilt behind,
I run where I cannot be found,
I seek to distract my mind
I don't listen, don't look around.
But it is a deafening sound,
I never heard anything so loud.

In order that I might remain sane,
I try to fill up my troubled brain
With major worldly affairs,
Business wheeling and dealing,
Financial endeavors and dares
Hoping they might do the healing.

But the voices adamantly persist
Awake, or asleep, or anywhere

They seem to obstinately insist
On haunting my soul everywhere.

So, please beat, beat the drums
To overpower the guilt noises.
Don't stop beating the drums
To subdue my past sinful choices.

Beat them loud, beat the drums
To hush up my overbearing fear
Beat them hard, beat the drums,
So I will not be able to hear
What I do not want to hear.

Which Road Leads to the Avenue of Light?

"And this is the judgment, that the light has come into the world, and men loved darkness rather than light, because their deeds were evil. For everyone who does evil hates the light, and does not come to the light, lest his deeds should be exposed."

(John 3:19,20)

"I don't want to change. This is the way I am, and this is who I will always be. It is my genetic makeup and cultural heritage and no one can do anything about it. As a matter of fact, my pride preserves me from change. I hold on to my pride to resist any change even if it were for the better. My identity stems from stagnation and I will not allow anyone to tamper with my right to stay exactly where I am.

"You may introduce me to freedom, but I will run away from it. You may offer guidance to the Avenue of Light, but I will advertently go the opposite direction. I will prove myself by abiding by my beliefs, the good and the bad; it does not matter as long as I can claim that **they are mine, not borrowed from**

anyone, especially you."

You may have encountered people with this frame of mind. They repeat the statement, "I will not be like you," over and over just to claim their right for individuality. Pride is the key word here, and bigotry and intolerance are the outcome of it. A "bigot" is a narrow-minded, prejudiced person who holds blindly and intolerantly to a particular dogma, opinion, etc. This kind of ideology gives the right to its advocates to divide the world into two camps: "Us" and "Them." And of course, "Us" is a better breed than "Them." So, all the "Us's" form a united front to defeat all the "Thems" regardless of whether they are good or bad.

The atrocity launched against humanity on September 11, 2001, exemplified the conflict between "Us" and "Them;" it demonstrated how dangerous this attitude could be for all humanity. It also showed that traversers of this rugged road don't head to the direction of God's light. When the terrorists were certain that heaven was their reward, we wondered about their horrible fate. Like a moth, some people run full speed in the wrong direction towards a "false" light – only to get burned, experience excruciating pain, and bitterly project that onto others.

Could the warmth of God's love be the dissolver of pride and indifference?

Could God be the way leading to the true light?

The Mind of a Terrorist

Just because I hijacked a plane
That does not make me insane.
If you allow me to explain,
My motives will seem simple 'n plain.
So, if you want to understand me,
Examine carefully my history.

Since my early childhood,
I was taught to hate with a passion
My parents said I should
Harm the enemy without compassion.

They fostered darkness in my heart,
And convinced me it was smart.
I even adopted a kind of conviction
That endorsed killing without restriction.

They told me there were two groups:
Mine, then all those who oppose,
Against the latter, I should gather my troops
Attack 'n inflict harm without any remorse.

Till this day, I don't think it's awful
To murder; I consider it my right.
In my mind, it's justified and lawful
'Cause I was born to shed blood and fight.

I will sacrifice my life for my cause
Of spilling hatred; I will not hesitate,
I am really determined because
I am not scared to meet my dark fate.

I am taught that before I die
It's OK to hurt the innocent,
As long as,
To my inner darkness, I comply
And to my bitterness I give consent.
Till my last breath, I will try
To obliterate the enemy, it's my intent
Even if I didn't have a chance to repent.

I will offer myself as a sacrifice
For a mission planned in hell.
Yes, I pay a very high price
But some victims will live to tell.

My god is so vengeful 'n merciless
Who demands human sacrifice 'n revenge.
So, I will please him regardless
Of how much pain, on you, I'll impinge.

Over the years I developed pride,
To my enemies' rules, I will not abide.
Even if they were for the best,
I would continue to complain 'n protest.

My traditions and heritage
Tied me down in bondage.

When I failed to be free,
Your freedom deeply offended me
So, from my bondage cell,
I decided to turn your life into hell.

Yes, you may be free of bitterness,
But I'll use mine to destroy your life.
Yes, you may not be living in darkness,
But I'll use mine to activate my strife.
My acts will be my people's heritage,
'N I'm not sorry they're to your disadvantage.

You may call me a terrorist,
But I consider myself a martyr.
It's hatred at work, at its best
That you fear to face or encounter.

Stop Beating Your Head Against the Wall

"For the word of the cross is folly to those who are perishing, but to us who are being saved it is the power of God."

(1 Corinthians 1:18)

How confusing is it to look around and realize that you are the only one who really wants to live for God?

How disappointing to find out that Christianity has been reduced to represent organizations or communities to which you belong and you are considered one of the elites?

What a shame to transform a life-giving relationship between God and His children into a dry set of customs or social events practiced on Sundays and special occasions at church?

How disturbing when you observe people following a mirage in a deserted land where the word of God has been substituted for the word of "man"?

Who do I follow? You may ask while looking around you and finding the blind leading the blind.

You try to speak up the truth about God based on His true word, but you hear the echo of your own voice. No one wants to listen. Each has his/her own way of worship that has excluded the presence of Jesus Christ. Feeling alone? Don't let the religious anomalies of people's beliefs discourage you! Stop beating your head against the wall; you'll be wasting your time and energy. Don't stay in the same dark place for too long; proceed in your worship following God's light. Go to the right place where God's standards, rather than man's, are considered. You think you're the only believer in town? I doubt it! When Jesus Christ died on the cross He had the whole humanity's salvation in mind. Just follow God's light, network with the right people, focus your energy on God, and live a life that glorifies Him. Maybe your light will lead others to the truth.

Am I the Only Believer in Town?

Am I the only believer in town,
Or the only child of the Most High?
Why can't anybody see my crown,
Or see God's light as they pass by?

When I talk about God's grace,
They mock me right to my face.
They say, "We beg your pardon!
That is just your Christian jargon,
But we have our own faith
That does not need any grace,
We earn it by what we do,
We are not lazy like you!"

When I talk about salvation,
They question my inclination.
They say, "Who do you think you are?
We are much better than you by far,
Christianity is our religion,
So what exactly is your mission?"

I talk about the world around us
And how they need to know Jesus.
They say,
"We have enough congregation,
We don't need more complications.

We have our closed community,
We don't like to leave our vicinity,
It is very dangerous out there
So, we decided not to really care."

When I talk about the poor,
They say, "They self-destruct,
For them, there will never be a cure
Whether you give money or instruct.
It has been their fashion always
To relapse to their old ways
Of drugs, theft, and drinking;
Their ship is always sinking."

When we talk about God's word,
We are not exactly in accord.
They say,
"The Lord, we really seek
On Sundays every week.
We listen to a good preacher,
Who is our guide and teacher.
His sermons are always the best
So we go home and get to rest.
Why should we look up a verse,
Or, about the Bible, converse?"

They live a life of complacency
Marked with self-sufficiency.
They don't know they excluded the Lord
When they didn't know or read His word.
And alone, I am standing here
Hoping, my voice, they'll hear.

Alone, I can't help but wonder
About what category I'm under.

**Am I the only believer in town,
Or the only child of the Most High?
Why can't anybody see my crown.
Or see His light when they pass by?**

Stay Where You Are!

"This people honors Me with their lips, but their heart is far from Me; in vain do they worship Me, teaching as doctrines the precepts of man."
(Matthew 15:8,9)

The train going to eternal life continually passes by where you are. People around you get on that train and proceed with their life towards one destination, eternal life.

It's your choice then. If you would like to join the bandwagon, know that Jesus Christ has paid the price on the cross. But if you refuse to go on that trip, just do not move; **stay where you are!**

If you want to stay in a dark place while others approach the light, **stay where you are!**

If you're satisfied with the familiar status quo, then be satisfied with just going to church, don't attempt to have a relationship with God, don't pray, and don't read His word. **Just stay where you are!**

If you insist on limiting your belief to the historical story of Jesus Christ while you see others' faith in Jesus Christ blossom and heal their souls, **stay where you are?**

If you want to live according to the worldly desires of your carnal body while others experience a new creation in Christ, **stay where you are!**

If you want to quench the Holy Spirit and live in the flesh while pretending you're not, **stay where you are!**

If you want to be fruitless while others produce the fruit of the Spirit of love, joy, peace, and kindness, **stay where you are!**

If you insist on being lazy refusing to use your talents while others invest in them and make profit, **just stay where you are!**

If you want to limit yourself to one group of people while others expand and reach out for people from all walks of life to love, serve, and witness to, Just do nothing but go to church, and **stay where you are!**

If you want to live vicariously on the good faith of others while failing to have your own, **stay where you are!**

If it is your choice to live a shallow life speaking the Christian jargon without understanding the real meaning of salvation, **stay where you are!**

If you want to face tribulations alone while others depend on the Lord and rejoice in their suffering knowing that it produces endurance and hope, **stay where you are!**

If you insist on harboring a grudge that cripples you while others are having no problem forgiving and moving on, **stay where you are!**

If you want to live in bondage allowing the world to dictate its code on you while others are liberated in Christ, **stay where you are!**

If you wish to carry your burden and worries on your shoulder while others cast theirs at the foot of the cross, **stay where you are!**

If you want to miss the train heading to eternal life, **stay**

where you are!

But if your desire is to head to the Kingdom of Heaven, stop being sluggish, take a step forward, open the door of your heart, and allow Jesus Christ to save your life and grant you His love and grace. Then, you can honor Him with your life when you work out your salvation with fear and trembling.

They JUST Go to Church

Some people work out their faith
With trembling and God's fear,
They understand the word "grace,"
The person of Christ, they endear.

Others **JUST** go to church
To satisfy an imperative urge
Thinking by going to church,
Their souls will be purged.

For them, spirituality is a show
So to church, they get ready 'n go.
They get a sort of spiritual high
That allows them to get by.

With absolutely no convictions,
They sedate their conscience.
With absolutely no devotion,
They **JUST** go with the motion.

JUST going to church, for them,
Is a social and public game,
But the unbelief within them,
Remains almost always the same.

They like to stay where they are,
Their hearts do not go very far,
Shallow they like to remain,
From sin, they do not abstain.
Their moral code is in a gutter,
You confront them, they stutter.
They don't know right from wrong
And
They've been churchgoers for so long.

While some people learn and grow,
Others' progress is really slow,
Salvation,
They don't comprehend or know
They **JUST** go with the flow.

When it's time for communion,
They step forward to partake
While their dear life companion,
They mistreat and forsake.

In life some people proceed
Knowing Jesus Christ, indeed
While others remain stagnant
Having absolutely no intent
To respond to God's urgent call;
They tend to hesitate and stall.

While some strife to win the race,
Others adamantly refuse to have faith.
Some willingly receive God's grace

That others completely fail to embrace,
So they **JUST** get a spiritual high
JUST to allow them to get by,
But they have no realization
Of the concept of salvation.

As the years pass and go by,
They don't even attempt or try
To approach the redeeming light;
They remain in their dark site.
Even though it's within their grasp
Light trickles off their clasp.

Some people move on and progress
While others decline and regress.

Time Does Not Wait

"Look carefully then how you walk, not as
unwise men but as wise, making the most of the
time, because the days are evil."
(Ephesians 5:15,16)

Cicadas are insects that live only in the eastern part of the United States. Cicadas live in the ground and then come out once every 17 years. So if you really want to see them, you'll have to watch your calendar because they live for only six weeks above the ground.

Some events in our life are like that. They only happen once in a blue moon, or even once in a lifetime. If we are not alert enough, we might miss the whole show and live to regret it.

Some precious moments are not redeemable once they pass by:

watching your little ones grow,
sharing happy moments with your loved ones,
helping a friend in a crisis,
taking care of your loved ones when they're sick,
doing any good deed while you have a chance, and
forgiving those who wronged you before it's too late.

Time doesn't wait for us. Once a moment of time is gone, it belongs to the past and you can't retrieve it except through your memory. It is really a choice to make any given moment a source of good or bad memory. Like pieces of a big puzzle, the moments in our life can create a picture. It is up to us to make this picture glowing with contentment and satisfaction, or sadness and regrets.

It's Too Late

He beckoned me to his side
And draped his arms around me.
He said, "Come, stay by my side,"
Then whispered words so lovingly.

Then the telephone rang,
And, to his office he sprang.
It was his business partner
Discussing an urgent matter.
He closed his office door
'N for the rest of the day,
I saw his face no more.
I guess I could honestly say
It was a short *rendez-vous*
That was for sure past due.
But with his schedule as it is,
Our little date, he had to miss.

He promised his little daughter
He would accompany her
To her first piano recital.
To her, it was really vital
For her daddy to attend;
He was like her best friend.
He prepared his camcorder
To tape his beloved daughter.

But the telephone rang
To his office he sprang.
He closed his office door,
And for the rest of the day,
She saw his face no more.
I guess she can honestly say
It was too good to be true.
It was time for her to construe
Her big daddy wouln't be able
To attend 'cause he was unavailable.

His very old and sick mother
Beseeched him to visit her
While she was in the hospital;
She was sick and it was critical.
He hastened to his dear mother,
He really wanted to comfort her.
He brought her a lovely bouquet
He assured her she would be OK.

But his cell phone rang
And off he sprang.
He said it was an emergency,
He had to go to his agency.

He came back the next day,
But to his surprise and dismay
The lovely flowers were dead,
His mom was not in her bed.

He cried, "Too late, too late!

For me, death couldn't wait.
I could have waited there,
I could have bid her good-bye,
I shouldn't have gone anywhere,
I did not even bother try.
Yes, I succeeded in my deal,
But now I honestly feel
What was the big deal?"

Self-Preservation

"I have been crucified with Christ; it is no longer I who live, but Christ Who lives in me; and the life I now live in the flesh I live by faith in the Son of God."

(Galatians 2:20)

The word "to preserve" means "to keep from harm, damage, danger, or evil." To preserve food is to add a preservative so it can protect it from getting spoiled. Every species self-preserves, each in a different way. When some animals are cornered, they attack. When others sense impending danger, they run away. Some are parasites living at the expense of others.

Man was made in a different way, though. First, he was made in the image of God. Second, he was made to live for God. One characteristic that is exclusive to man is having a free will to choose right from wrong. Some people choose to self-preserve by adopting a selfish life style grabbing and snatching what is not theirs. They also try to fill the void in their heart by hoarding and refusing to give whatever they have.

The latter kind of people are under the impression that whatever they do, they do to protect themselves from the mighty darts of the evil world. They have an urge to keep provisions because they feel they are in a state of emergency.

However, they get themselves trapped in a vicious cycle of more greed, more grabbing, and more self-centeredness. To their surprise, the more they take from the world, the more they feel the void inside of them because this "stuff" that they accumulate is the wrong choice for them. Man was made to live for God and God's ways are far different from man's ways. The only way for man to self-preserve is to be in union with his Creator through accepting Jesus Christ's act on the cross for his salvation. It is an interesting concept though. To self-preserve in Jesus Christ, means living for Him rather than living for oneself. The **"I"** has to be crossed out and replaced by "Jesus Christ." When we surrender our life to our Lord Jesus Christ's will, He becomes our **Protector and Provider** in the world so we would not perish. In Him, we become a new creation that will be granted to live forever with God in His Kingdom of Heaven.

I Am Not Selfish

You say, "You're so selfish
It's just simple and pure,
Your conduct is so childish
It shows how you're insecure.
For your greed and anguish,
There is no simple cure."

But
I want you to understand
When I was still too little
Our home was built on sand,
It collapsed little by little
So all I got was second-hand,
Even **love** was worn out 'n brittle.

I felt lonely and detached
I longed to be attached.
When people shunned me away,
I longed for things to own.
I invited a habit to stay
That I've never outgrown.

I learned to grab and snatch
To fill the hole formed inside,
But I could only patch
The wound from the outside.

I know
I acted beneath your expectation,
And created my bad reputation.
Sorry, I didn't win your admiration,
But it was for self-preservation.

Because of what I say 'n do,
You think, myself, I adore.
I tell you, you have no clue
What I usurp and grab for.

I want to love and cherish
My spirit, wounded 'n scarred,
It's an attempt to not perish
In this loveless world; it's hard.

Yet,
In the process I didn't get
What I longed to obtain.
My soul could not rest,
My anguish, I couldn't sustain.

When **love** came along my way,
I could not invite it in.
I failed to convince it to stay
In the emptiness within.
Love, you can't grab and snatch
Like an object you can possess.
When you finally meet your match,
You have to care for and caress.

45

Because I felt I didn't belong,
I didn't use my heart for so long,
It accumulated debris and dust
That debilitated me to trust.
I lacked the ability to give
I chose a selfish life to live.

I know
I acted beneath your expectation
And created my bad reputation.
Sorry, I didn't win your admiration,
But it was for self-preservation.

I Am Not Supposed to Make Mistakes

"Blessed is he whose transgression is forgiven, whose sin is covered. Blessed is the man to whom the Lord imputes no inequity, and in whose spirit there is no deceit."

(Psalms 32:1,2)

Part of being a human being is to make mistakes and to realize that we are fallible. A true believer in the holiness of God would see how dark he or she is compared to the purity and holiness of God. Once we come to this realization, there is no way for us to feel proud of our good deeds because we realize that we are not equipped with the ability to be perfect.

Some parents are bringing up their children to seek perfection in whatever they are doing. However, when this approach is taken to the extreme form, it could be counterproductive. Feeling the need for God to help them seek perfection starts to be replaced by the feeling that "I am already perfect!" This attitude is the beginning of a host of what I call, **"the guilt-bondage syndromes."**

Let's take the example of people who constantly lie; one lie should be told to cover another. When friends confront them with their lies, they have a pattern that they follow and it stems

47

from their guilt: the kind of **"toxic guilt"** that is mixed with shame. **Shame** has the ability to convince people that they made a mistake because of their **"bad self;"** how bad they really are. Shame scrutinizes the character to the core to the extent that it does not give room for repentance. A person suffering from this "toxic guilt" or "the guilt-bondage syndrome" may feel entrapped in his guilt because of his distorted thought, "If I am really guilty, then that means that I am really beyond repair and thus, I cannot even repent."

So to defend himself or herself, someone who is under that category and who has not experienced the love and forgiveness of God, may make **cognitive appraisals** that may lead to this course of action:

First, exaggerating the ugliness of the offense.

Second, denying making the horrible mistake, and thus, denying one's own fallibility.

Third, allowing this "toxic guilt" to make one avoid repentance.

Fourth, not owning up to one's mistake, turning the table around, and giving the accuser the guilt trip, "I can't believe I did this horrible thing. How dare you put me in such a bind and make me feel so terrible."

Where "toxic guilt" leads to self-condemnation, denial, blame, and a reprobate soul, **"benign guilt"** leads to repentance and forgiveness. Let us follow this conversation:

Mary: When you said you didn't have money, that was not the truth.

John: Oh Mary, yes, I lied to you and I really regret it. Can you forgive me? What can I do to correct my mistake?

For a free person who has experienced God's forgiveness, Four things are happening in John's heart:

First, feeling guilty.

Second, admitting one's mistakes and thus, admitting one's fallibility.

Third, using this healthy guilt to seek repentance.

Fourth, owning up to one's own mistake and trying to make amends.

Guilt is necessary for repentance, but the question is which kind of guilt, "toxic guilt," or "benign guilt?"

Friends Don't Lie to Each Other

You really hurt me my friend.
After 20 years of alleged friendship,
I finally discovered it was the end
Of our so-called friendly relationship.

Friends don't lie to each other,
Don't play games and manipulate,
Don't get jealous of one another,
Yet show a phony front, so great.

Friends don't talk behind your back
And, your character, they don't attack.
They don't send your reputation to the gutter,
Just that they may feel they are better.
"Au contraire," and on the other hand,
Of all the people, they should understand
That love, patience, and kindness,
Friends, should exemplify.
Your faithfulness and goodness,
They should exalt and magnify.

So,
When I reached the end of my rope
And I ran out of any hope,
I decided not to pretend
That you were a good friend.

I discarded the appeasing front
And finally decided to confront
You with all the games played,
And the innocent front displayed.
But when I told you, you lied,
With all your might, you denied.
Instead of dealing with it regrettably,
You denied everything vehemently.
You didn't feel remorse, instead,
The truth, you intentionally, did bend.
Alas, you accused me of daring
To confront you with the truth, so sad,
You accused me of not caring,
And not concealing what's really bad.

Your falsehood created a huge wall
Of impassiveness and indifference.
Surly, we both felt so small
In the face of this intolerance.
I was hoping that our Christianity
Would mend this bitter reality.

In the end, the bad guy, I turned to be
'Cause, your mistakes, you refused to see.
Even if I forgave your inadequacy,
Even if I put up with your fantasy,
The situation would not progress
Because,
Your mistakes, you refuse to confess.
And alas,
You won't allow our Christianity
To correct 'n mend this bitter reality.

Who Do I Reflect?

"And if you are sure you are a guide to the blind,
a light to those who are in darkness, a corrector
of the foolish, a teacher of children, having in
the law the embodiment of knowledge and truth
– you then who teach others, will you not teach
yourself?"

(Romans 2:19-21)

Mahandas Gandhi, leader of the Indian nationalist movement against the British rule, had expressed that if it hadn't been for the Christians, he would have become a Christian. What a powerful statement from one of the most prominent peace advocates in the twentieth century! Remember, Mahandas Gandhi was the one who said, "The candle of nonviolence should be able to burn even when the cyclone of violence surrounds it." What a great concept adopted and lived by a non-Christian leader.

The question now is, what have we done to Christianity? The most beautiful teachings of Jesus Christ are just read in the Bible, but they are far from being lived. As Christians, we are supposed to be the mirror that reflects Christ in His love, kindness, compassion, wisdom, and meekness. But are we really reflecting all that?

I guess when we deviate from Christ, the source of righteousness, our "so-called righteousness" will be tinted with the colors of the world and the real righteousness may lose its glow. We have to beware of the **virtue dimmers** in life such as extreme practicality, busyness, love of money and power, and selfishness. They are dimmers because they are supported by the world. But as we draw near God, we can reclaim our status as **"the light of the world."** The only catch is that we cannot shine away from the eternal light, Jesus Christ. We have to draw our energy, warmth, and illumination from Him. Then maybe we can say, "The candle of righteousness should be able to burn even when the cyclone of unrighteousness surrounds it."

To My Surprise

I really pity my coworker,
To her, everything's a tearjerker.
When a trivial thing goes wrong,
She expects me to go along
And acknowledge her "feeling"
Which, to me, is really unappealing.
So when she gets that melodramatic,
I just refuse to be sympathetic.

The other day she was crying
Because her dog was dying.
I said, "Please, be practical,
A dog is just an animal."
I refused to be sympathetic
'Cause I thought it was pathetic.

Another time she sat, forlornly,
With flowing tears, unabated
She said she felt so lonely
Her only son had instigated
The idea of moving out of town
Which made her feel down.

I wondered about her impracticality
I thought she'd lost touch with reality.

Sons should grow up to be men,
And that shouldn't cause chagrin.

Once she asked in a tone, formidable
She was in dire need of a favor,
She asked if I would kindly be able
To drive her and her sick neighbor
To "the not so far away" clinic
'Cause she was afraid she would panic.
I advised her to take Dial-a-Ride,
She didn't need me by her side.

I pitied her emotional instability,
So, I talked to her about Jesus
And how He restores stability
To our life and how He loves us.
I tried to sincerely urge her
To take a heightened urgency
In becoming His daughter
It was like a state of emergency.

To my distress and my surprise,
She looked at me pitifully,
And told me, "You don't realize
I've considered that very carefully,
But when I look at your apathy,
Lack of warmth, lack of empathy,
I can't buy your phony religion
So, I kind of made a decision,
I decided never to become like you
If it would make me that untrue."

To my distress and my surprise,
She didn't thank me effusely
I guess I failed to realize
My apathy had hurt her profusely.

Feeling Sorry for Others

"Rejoice with those who rejoice, weep with those who weep."

(Romans 12:15)

"Feeling sorry for others" is a "good" feeling that, in some cases, can gratify our ego. When we are in tune with people's adversities, we may get the impression that we are one step ahead of them and that may enhance our sense of superiority.

Think about it, people who live vicariously on other people's misfortune tend to spread bad news much faster than they spread good news. Or better, good news may not circulate at all. That may be due to the misconception that if the world were topsy-turvy, the mediocre situation of some people's existence would be justified. By comparison, their world may seem bright coexisting next to the dark outside world. Of course, you can depict the underlying sense of jealousy.

So, beware when you are happy and wish to share your bliss! Your so-called friends, who gave their allegiance to you at your dejected state, might disappear in the joyous sound of your good fortune.

However, if the love of God is poured into our hearts from the right source, the Holy Spirit, then this encompassing love can be reflected onto others. It could be expressed without any reservation in all situations. This is the true kind of genuine love from above that we are meant to share with others

True or Fake

It was a bright sunny morning
I was full of pleasant aspiration
Until I heard the doctor proclaiming
My bad health and condemnation.

I gazed and shrank in my chair
Struck with regret and despair.
My tears streamed down my face,
For me, it was the end of the race.
My health was no longer there,
I was young and it was not fair.

I left with a heavy-laden heart,
Did not know where to start.
My fingers found their way
To a telephone in the hallway,
I dialed the number of my friend
Her listening ear, she did lend.
My friend came in a hurry,
She assured me not to worry.
I said, "That's it for me!"
She replied, "I don't agree!"
For with all the loved ones I had,
Things weren't going to be bad
They can give me my strength
To persevere 'n regain my health.

Evidently, that was truly the case,
They were always by my side,
They brightened my darkest days,
Made my struggle a smooth ride.

Then my luck turned around
I became really well and about.
It seemed like a riddle
To become fit as a fiddle.
I lucked out, regained my health,
And God granted me great wealth.
I was doing extremely well
I was happy I was alive to tell.

However,
Those who were my lifesavers
Were all fresh out of favors,
The news of my speedy success
Apparently scared them away,
It's funny, when I was a mess,
By my side, they wanted to stay.
The news of my misfortune
Spread around everywhere,
But watching my good fortune
Evidently, they cannot bear.
The thought my life was bliss,
They like to avoid and dismiss.

I guess
They wanted to give me strength
In my sickness but not in health,

True friends, they had been
But not through thick and thin.

In the midst of my worst fears
I could see their genuine tears,
But seeing my joy and laughter,
They couldn't have run away faster.

My good fortune, they can't take
Would that make them true or fake?

The Missing Invention

*"Put on then, as God's chosen ones, holy and
beloved, compassion, kindness, lowliness,
meekness, and patience, forebearing one
another."*

(Colossians 3:12,13)

The 20th Century had witnessed the greatest discoveries and inventions in the history of humanity. As if all the genius minds of the century had collaborated to bring about comfort, beauty, health, convenience, peace, freedom, and victory to all mankind. If we go down the memory lane and follow some of the accomplishments, we'll marvel at the human mind and it's capacity.

As we entered the century, electricity had illuminated this new era of discoveries. Yes, we have light to help us see our way at night, but **can this light illuminate our souls?**

In the field of communication, before the turn of the century, in 1876, the first one-way-message on the telephone was sent. And in 1928, we witnessed the birth of one of the most powerful media in history, television. The purpose was to have better communication. **But do we really know how to communicate** knowing that one of the main reasons for divorce is bad communication?

When we talk about transportation that was surely the beginning of the automotive and aviation age. The purpose was to help us go places faster and easier. Yes, we sure go places, **but are they the right places? Did these inventions help our souls develop a better sense of direction?**

In the 1900s, not only could we look inside the human body using the X-Ray, but also inside our psyche. That was the time when Sigmund Freud had published his book *The Interpretation of Dreams.* Yes, now we know more about what goes on in our minds and bodies, **but do we really comprehend the yearning of our souls?**

In the medical field, this century had truly witnessed many breakthroughs starting from the development of penicillin to the transplantation of body organs. The purpose was to promote health and good quality of life. Yes, we may have managed to cure many diseases of the body, **but are our souls healed from within?**

Reaching high was the aim of the architects and astronauts of the century. Skyscrapers were built, and Neil Armstrong actually walked on the moon in 1969. Yes, we reached high places, **but why can't we reach Heaven?**

In 1945, the world witnessed the end of World War II and that was followed by the birth of a peace organization, the United Nations. In 1992 we witnessed the collapse of Communism. What else do we need to establish peace and stability? **But are we really free and at peace with ourselves?**

In the last century we were so busy converting the world with the great amenities we had. Now, we are comfortable, yet we are still busy on a daily basis wheeling and dealing and making money. We are so busy that we forgot the real important values in life, **caring and compassion** that no invention can provide to us.

We have had enough accomplishments to make us ecstatic. We have had enough trials to make us very strong. And we have experienced enough misery and sorrow to make us human.

The question is: are we ecstatic, strong, or even compassionate human beings? And if not, what kind of miraculous invention will we need in order to become that way? Would it be manmade or will we need the help of the Creator of all things, the Consoler of Our Souls, and the Manager of our minds and hearts?

I'm Sorry!
I Don't Have Time to Care

When she lost her loved one,
Around her, anguish, was spun
She was down and depressed
To me, she clearly expressed
She needed a real friend.
Thinking to myself, I said,
"She has friends and family
She doesn't really need me."
I looked in my appointment book,
And I gave her a leery look.
I wanted her to be aware,
I didn't have time to spare.
I said I was pressed with time,
And she considered it a crime.

Disappointed, her head she shook
My good intentions, she mistook.
Her own view, she proclaimed,
And with authority, she claimed,
"Your hard work is just an attempt
To run away from responsibility
You want to make yourself exempt
From showing care and availability.
You do not have time to spare

'Cause you don't wish to care."
Her accusations, I could not bear
'Cause I just have no time to care.

My next door friend and neighbor
Asked for a very urgent favor
I assured him,
"On me, you can always depend."
He waited for me and in the end
The appointment, I surely forgot,
I could have called, but I did not.
Does he expect me to drop
Everything 'n, my work, stop?
In what I do, I am meticulous,
To leave it just for him,
Would be kind of ridiculous.

I am too busy and occupied
It is really simple and plain.
But, no matter how hard I tried
It seemed impossible to explain
That, to me, time was worth money,
And I worked hard for every penny.

Well,
My daughter doesn't complain
She understands when I explain
That Mommy can't be everywhere
'Cause she has no time to spare.
I take her to the babysitter,
I come very late to get her.
I don't even brush her hair

'Cause I don't have time to care.

I agree with you, I have to confess
My house is a complete mess,
My cooking gets to be less 'n less.
But my husband is nonchalant
He takes us to a nice restaurant.
And talking about the garden
What's that? I beg your pardon!
Flowers? Who'd plant and water,
I, my husband, or my daughter?
The roses are kind of dead
It actually has been so long
Since I cared for them or fed.
It's a fact, be it right or wrong
I am busy and I am aware
I do not have time to care!

The Mind of a Bully

"But they did not obey or incline their ear, but walked in their own counsels and the stubbornness of their evil hearts, and went backward and not forward."

(Jeremiah 7:24)

The bully is someone who holds a position in life that says, "I am better than you, so I'll show you who the winner is. I will hurt you before you hurt me. It had better be my way!"

A bully is often full of anger towards life, other people, and more importantly, at himself. This anger is expressed in his/her resort to the fight instinct whether there's an impending danger or not. A bully feels good fighting because the world is perceived as a perilous place where we have to be on our guard ready to pounce and attack any time. So bullies flaunt their power and authority to ward off danger that is, most of the time, imaginary.

A bully is someone who, since his childhood, has never developed peace of mind because he was either bullied or controlled. As a result, he/she tends to constantly create turmoil for his/her life and others. That sure reflects the turmoil that exists in his/her threatened heart. However, believe it or not, it is self-preservation.

Living as victims for a long time, builds up resentment to the idea of being a victim. In turn, bullies prefer to victimize others in order to feel superior at the expense of others' inferiority. Is there hope for a bully? God's mercy and grace can demonstrate real love so anyone can see himself/herself as being placed in God's eternal loving heart. **Love is a healing force in life.** Observe someone who is in love; he becomes the most generous and giving person. Because love has the characteristic of multiplying, once we experience the value of love in our life, we can extend it to others. So bullies who are touched by God's love will have no reason whatsoever to put people down because they are "in love" with others and with the world. Most importantly, they know how to love God.

My Way or the Highway

In order to win the last round,
Early in life, I understood fully
One has to stand his ground
So, you manipulate like a bully.

I took after my father, of course
To me, he was the inspiring force.
He ruled us with a mighty iron hand,
His cruelty, we couldn't understand.
But we had to abide by his rules
'N we were the submissive fools.
I guess the message he did relay
Was, "My way or the highway!"

Since then I did some growing
Now, I am the all-knowing.
To my father, I hold a candle,
I like to fly over the handle
And act out like a true bully
To let people understand fully:
To no one, I will ever submit,
'N I won't ever allow or permit
Any one to make me the victim
Like I used to be with "him."
I sure follow my father's model
I feel safe when I cause trouble

'Cause a solemn oath I swore
The victim, I will be no more!

When my story will be told,
I would like all of you to know
How I manipulated 'n controlled,
And how I got to be like so.

I took after my father, of course
To me, he was the inspiring force,
And the message I want to relay
Is,
"It's either my way or the highway."

Who Is the Real Therapist?

*"I told you that you would die in your sins, for
you will die in your sins unless you believe that
I am He."*

(John 8:24)

In order for a baby to grow, it takes a collaborative effort. First, the right nourishment should be chosen. Then, somebody has to nurture him/her. Most importantly, the baby must accept this nourishment.

There is an interesting analogy that explains the meaning of therapy. In the Middle Ages, the idea of therapy was to take away the ailment. When someone was sick, the medicine man would come and place a wet towel on the hurt area of the body. The idea was to transfer the ailment from the body to the wet piece of cloth and to dry it up in the sun. Then the healing was believed to occur.

Four aspects had collaborated to consummate **the act of healing:** the presence of medicine (the piece of cloth), the presence of the medicine man, the patient's acceptance of the medicine, and the healing power of the sun. Which one of those aspects had facilitated the healing process? Which aspect had the healing power? Think about it. The medicine and the medicine man were the facilitators of the healing. However, without the patient's permission, healing could have never occurred. As for the healing power, it lied in the heat and warmth of the sun. The same concept can be applied to our spiritual growth. God, Who alone possesses the power to heal our souls, is eagerly waiting for everyone of us to open his/her heart and accept Him as Lord and Savior. God may use all the resources available to you to send you the message of the Gospel. He may use circumstances, people, or even problems to facilitate your growth. **Your role is to open the door of your heart and allow God to touch you with the warmth of His love and start the healing process in you.** The healing is not going to start without your permission.

Making a U-Turn

I went to the grocery store
And I met someone at the door.
She greeted me with great ardor,
And addressed me like a daughter,
"How are you Mrs. Samaan?
I am your student Suzanne!"
Then I remembered her little face
Back in my Sunday school days.
I was her third grade teacher
I sure was glad to meet her.

Naturally, I had a vested interest
To know her ins and outs
She said, "I have tried my best
But I was faced with doubts.
So, I did my keen investigation
On the cross, faith, and salvation,
But I discovered they were not in."
She said that with a broad grin.

She continued her talk carelessly,
About her life story, we conversed,
And I found out how aimlessly,
The wrong path, she had traversed.

Yes,
She went to Sunday school class,
But she did not get it, and alas,
She still holds on to her sin,
And she's empty from within.

There was something strange
And I had this burning concern
Wasn't she supposed to change,
Believe, repent, 'n make a U-turn?

After all these years of attendance,
She didn't declare her acceptance
Of Jesus Christ's act on the cross.
This is a shame and a great loss.
What a waste of time and energy
On the part of the laymen 'n clergy?
Didn't she hear their preaching?
'N what was the use of my teaching?
Wasn't I supposed to give inspiration
Sufficient to lead to her salvation?

Now, she is supposedly mature,
She seems irrational and insecure
Wandering aimlessly and alone
As if, the truth, she weren't shown.
She is wasting her precious youth,
Running away from the only truth.

And I still have a strong concern,
When will she make her U-turn,
Start anew, turn over a new leaf,

Cast away her doubts, and believe?
When will she admit and learn
That she has to make a U-turn?

A True Leader

"The greatest among you shall be your servant;
whoever exalts himself will be humbled,
and whoever humbles himself will be exalted."
(Matthew 23:11,12)

Leaders who are after earthly success are usually driven by **power, recognition, and greed.** They focus on the outcome instead of the process. So in the process of attaining success, they may allow themselves to turn into monsters and they eventually lose their loyalty to God. Drenched in their ploy to establish their authority, they soon forget that whether we are leaders or followers, we are called to be **servants.** We are called to forget the **"I"** and focus on God.

If the latter is our mission, then we have to fulfill God's commandment, "A new commandment I give to you, that you love one another; even as I have loved you, that you also love one another." (John 13:34, 35) Christ's love for us led Him to the cross to save us. But isn't He the Son of God? And who are we to assume a role above His.

A true leader should follow the model of Jesus Christ. He came to serve not to be served. He came to **inspire and to enable people to produce good results or good fruit.**

Jesus Christ wants to make us His disciples, and a true disciple follows his master's footsteps. However, Christ does not delegate responsibility and leave us alone to stumble. First, He set a good example for us when He humbled Himself, left His throne in Heaven, and came to earth to serve us. Second, He is still alive now and is more than willing to coach us and guide us in our path to obtaining a **servant heart.**

Arrogance Is
Perfect Material for a Miracle

Ready to kick up my heels,
I went after life's deals
With knock-the-walls-down attitude
I didn't care if I were nice or rude,
Didn't care for anybody's advice,
I wanted victory at any price.

My ultimate goal was to impress,
Myself first, with speedy success.
My mission, no one could derail,
I could not ever afford to fail.
So, I proceeded in full force
And I succeeded, of course.
However,
I paid the price of my success:
Regrets, pressure, and stress.

I created an atmosphere
Of unfriendliness and hostility
To all, it was perfectly clear,
Being boss meant royalty.
Even though no one agrees,
I like to subjugate my employees.

The more people were helpless,
The more I became ruthless.
I continued to slash and burn
Whatever came in the way,
So stress, was what I did earn
From the wrong foundation I lay,
"To stay on top of the ladder,
Nobody 'n nothing else did matter!"

But oh, the nights, so miserable
Over and over, I had to spend.
They were really intolerable
Even my success, couldn't mend.
I had tried every down pillow,
And every advice, I did follow.
But I couldn't have sleep 'n serenity
And that was my sad reality.

I guess my arrogant heart
Was ready for transformation,
I was game for a fresh start
To stop my sick domination.

I asked God to make me a servant
Instead of being an unjust master,
I wanted to stop being arrogant
And feel for others for a starter.
I tried to the best of my ability
To treat others with humility,
Instead of being haughty 'n sleek,
God taught me how to be meek.
That was not a new invention,

It was really God's intention.
I learned that it was a must
To earn my people's trust.
Who said that fostering hate,
Could build a company, so great?
I thought I was infallible,
I thought I was really smart,
I guess I needed a miracle
To transform my callous heart.

The Malignant Competition

"So put away all malice and all guile and insincerity and envy and all slander. Like newborn babes, long for the pure spiritual milk, that by it you may grow up to salvation; for you have tasted the kindness of the Lord."

(1Peter 2:1-3)

In this age of great accomplishments, people want to excel and climb ladders to the highest aspirations. Ambition is great when we're competing in the right direction. Often times we compare ourselves with others and we try to prove to the world that we are the best. That may be acceptable for the children of this world, but not for the children of God. That is for a simple reason. When we allow ourselves to be engulfed in the world's competing game, we also allow ourselves to feel jealousy if we're not the only topnotch in town. It becomes like a constant battle with the world and others over who can be the best of all. In this parody of jealous competition, some may adopt the slash and burn mentality and become like a malignant growth that is hungry to destroy anything in its way.

Three things may bring about this **malignant jealous competition:** worldly ambition, lack of thanksgiving, and the inability to love our neighbors as we love ourselves. The opposite of these three conditions comprises the antidote to the malignant jealous competition.

For example, if our ambition is mainly in the spiritual realm, and if whatever we do, we do to glorify God, then competition will take a different form. Instead of competing with others to become better than them, we compete with ourselves weighing our spiritual progress at the moment against our spiritual status in the past. The goal would be to ameliorate the quality of our life with God. Finally, if we wrap our worldly ambition with our spiritual ambition, then our goal will become to glorify God in whatever we do.

With this in mind, God's commandments will be engraved in my soul. According to Jesus the greatest commandment of all is to love God with all our hearts and to love our neighbors as we love ourselves. By fulfilling this commandment, jealousy disappears because what I would wish for myself I can also wish for my neighbor.

Thanksgiving wraps the package of the antidote to the malignant jealous competition bottle. Living a thanksgiving life and thanking God for whatever we got from the bundle of life, showers our life with contentment that can replace jealousy, the one thing that destroys friendship and, most of all, the thankful heart.

I Am Not Jealous

I am not jealous, in fact
I want my life to be intact.
I wish to shine and succeed
I am one of those very few ·
Who have this urge and need
To excel 'n be better than you.

My strategy when I compete
Is to badmouth you at the core.
For my success to be complete,
I establish a very close rapport
With your indifferent enemy
The aim is
To destroy you and exalt "me."

My ins and outs, I do not say,
Information, I don't give away
Lest you use it in your endeavor
To ameliorate and become better.

You wonder about my curious inquiry
About your life, 'n my snooping around,
I excavate your dirty laundry,
Any scandal that could be found.
The aim is
To hold back your speedy success

And feel that you are less 'n less.
I am distressed when you succeed,
And you assert, I am jealous.
Your progress, I'd like to impede,
And you consider it mere malice.

You say, I am in your space,
I'm telling you, it's fair game.
If you were in my exact place,
You would surely do the same.

You see
If you want to climb the ladder,
Nothing else will ever matter.
To your own good 'n well being
You will give first priority
Then, you will be agreeing
That others' pitiful inferiority
Can enhance your superiority.

I'm not jealous, in fact,
I want my life to be intact.
I wish to shine and succeed
I am one of those very few
Who have this urge and need
To excel 'n be better than you.

The Condescending Heart

"God opposes the proud, but He gives grace to the humble."

(James 4:6)

It was said, "A problem well-stated is a problem half solved." It is half solved because the next logical step would naturally be tackling the issue and finding solutions. But let's say we can pinpoint a bad situation, but refuse to admit the problem, and continue living as if there were no problem. What word comes to your mind when you witness this situation: denial, foolishness, avoidance, laziness, or cowardice?

An ordinary human being is capable of problem solving provided that he can pinpoint the problem. The person with a higher level of intelligence is the one who can detect problems and even anticipate them so they would be avoided in the future. However, realizing a bad situation and then refusing to correct it because of laziness, pride, or mere stubbornness, is a very primitive way of mental functioning. An example of the latter condition is to refuse to apologize for your wrongdoing.

An apology is a declaration of the heart that an erroneous act has taken place and that it shouldn't have occurred. A sincere apology declares three things, and works in three dimensions of time. First, it shows regret of what had happened in the past. Second, it demonstrates good intentions regarding the correction of the wrongdoing in the present. Third, it brings assurance that it will not happen again in the future.

By the same token, refusing to apologize declares three things, and works in three dimensions of time. First, it justifies the mistakes of the past and shows no remorse or responsibility. Second, it shows no intention whatsoever to correct the wrong doing in the present. Third, it instills an atmosphere of distrust because of the possibility that the wrong deed might reoccur in the future.

Refusing to apologize is like refusing to admit you are a sinner and that we are all liable to make mistakes. Beware because insisting on living in denial and declining repentance is an act of defiance against God. Failing to repent equals failing to draw near God. If you realize that God is light and sin is darkness, and that there is no companionship between the two, then you will understand. In order to live in God's light you have to discard your condescending attitude and confess your sins whether they were committed toward God or toward people.

I Will Not Apologize

You tell me,
"You refuse to say you're sorry
For your major imperfections.
For that, I honestly worry
About your petty convictions."

But
I **AM NOT** going to apologize
And, my integrity, jeopardize.
So, I choose to be bright
And pretend I am always right.

Let's iron up our differences.
You want me to say I'm erroneous
And to give up my main defenses,
'N I think it's a bit sanctimonious.

For someone who's condescending
What message will I be sending?
That I am less in stature
Than your perfect majesty?
Should I, my ego, fracture
And do away with my vanity?

Please, soften your approach
It makes you more palatable.

On my territory don't encroach
I'm telling you, it's not viable.

Whatever wrong I commit or say,
You can get over, it'll go away.
But to strip me off my only defense,
Is a kind of first-degree offense.
It is a well-known moral law
The helpless, you can't declaw.
If you cause my defenses to crumble,
My shaky self-image will fumble.

To me
It's a flagrant abuse of authority
To disparage and to humiliate
Someone for his petty inequity
When he's in his sorry state.
Go ahead, prove your false piety
But my image, I won't obliterate!

If you confront me with my mistake,
I will deny it vehemently
Disgrace, I cannot possibly take
I will fight you relentlessly.

So,
Don't you ever dare fantasize,
To you, I will ever apologize.
You just can't fathom or realize
That, that could lead to my demise.

The Arrogant Heart

*"The man of haughty looks and arrogant heart
I will not endure."*

(Proverbs 101:3)

We all have been forgiven by a merciful God Who sent His only begotten Son to die for our sins and grant us salvation. For that, we should be indebted for the rest of our lives. We were forgiven, so, don't you ever forget that!

When we live according to this fact, we ought to accept God's forgiveness for us with thanksgiving and pass it on to our fellow people. If God, the Holder of the universe Who is holy and without blemish, can forgive His creation, then by all means we have to show mercy to our fellow human beings.

If we follow God's model, forgiveness becomes an act of magnanimity towards people who do us wrong whether they have remorse or not. Our motto should be what Jesus Christ said on the cross, "Father, forgive them; for they know not what they do." (Luke 23:34)

Failing to forgive others in general is to place ourselves in a much higher status than theirs; a status that we cannot possibly claim as human beings. In God's sight we are all sinners in need for His grace and mercy for our salvation.

Failing to accept an apology in particular reflects the condition of a heart that is self-righteous, judgmental, arrogant, and impenitent that either hasn't experienced God's forgiveness, or isn't grateful for receiving it. This heart is in dire need to be exposed in the light of God to be able to see the extent of its darkness before it casts stones on other sinners. Maybe then it will humble itself and have mercy on others.

You Pierced My Heart with Your Apology

My friend, please hear me out,
When conflict was here 'n about,
I was alarmed, but I did not
Give you the benefit of the doubt.
Instead, a tone of animosity, I set,
The hurt was deep, I lost my grip,
And I fouled up our relationship.

I accused you vehemently, my friend
I misunderstood every word you said,
Your intentions, I completely misread,
And my hurt multiplied in the end.

Even though you were not wrong,
However, it didn't take you so long.
To explain your lucid point of view
Which I chose to misconstrue.
Nevertheless, you apologized humbly,
And I was touched immeasurably.
This lowly act of expiation
Has pierced my heart beyond belief
It wasn't met with appreciation
Because it didn't give me any relief.

It was beyond my heart's ability
To fathom this magnanimity.
It made me feel I was so little
Especially with a heart, so brittle.

I practically leapt to my feet
In astonishment and surprise,
But, your apology, I didn't greet
'Cause I refused to compromise.

I did not have an inkling
How humble and good you are.
In my heart I gave you a ranking
So high that was fit for a star.
Yet, I kept on holding a grudge,
An inch, I did not want to budge.

It was easier for me to be right
And, your character, scrutinize.
I have fought with all my might
To be the victim, 'Cause otherwise
I'd give in and let you win the fight.

Sorry, my friend
Your penance wasn't accepted
And your apology was sure rejected
'Cause I want to be right and prove
Your character is beyond repair,
Your piety, I wish to reprove
So, my precision, I can declare.

Running Away from Warmth

"And this is the judgment, that the light has come into the world, and men loved darkness rather than light, because their deeds were evil."

(John 3:19)

The sun, the source of light and warmth, is very crucial to the growth of all living things on earth. It is true that some organisms such as termites and certain kinds of fish are not exposed to the light and warmth of the sun; however, they could have never survived hadn't it been for the fact that their food is composed of materials or other organisms that are exposed to the light such as trunks of trees and ocean plants.

Statistics show that the rate of suicide escalates drastically in countries where there is no morning light continuously for several months. Some people experience seasonal depression when it is foggy or gloomy and light therapy is their option to regain their vivacious self. This reminds me of a story that I heard in Sunday school. It is about a young man who felt rejected by the cold, insipid people in his town that he decided to commit suicide by jumping in the river. However, on his way to the river, he said to himself that if he met anybody who would take notice of him as a human being, he would turn back. The story ends with an inquiry, "Suppose this somebody had been you, would he have turned back? Would your warm look have given sunshine to this lonely young man?"

On the emotional level, love and warmth are irreplaceable values for the survival of human beings and even animals. Isn't it amazing to know that babies can actually die if they are not touched or caressed? However, it doesn't become a mystery when we realize that God is love and that He created each one of us intricately with the utmost love and care. This is how we were designed: creatures who cannot be separated from the light and warmth on the physical level as well as the emotional level.

What a shame seeing people advertently running away from the warmth of their own feelings and the warm expressions of their fellow human beings. Their goal is to replace vulnerability with insipidness so they avoid feeling weak. So, off they proceed in life incessantly shoving their feelings aside and living in their bodies forgetting about their souls. In doing so, they work excessively, and plan their schedule so they wouldn't have a free moment to be alone with themselves. Alas, they choose to live apart from the light and warmth of God.

Iceman

Where are you Iceman?
I just talked to you here
You froze and away you ran.
What is it that you fear?
Tell me the truth if you can.

Are you young or old?
Tell me your story,
Or it hasn't been told.
Afraid the details are gory,
Or they'll mess up your world?
Inform me Iceman
I will help if I can.

Why aren't you nice?
Why are you so cold?
I understand
In order to be made of ice,
And remain in this mold,
Emotions, you put on hold.
What a pity, and whose advice?
Tell me
To whom, your soul, you sold?
I'm quite sure you paid a price
So dear as the price of gold

Your fears you suppressed,
Your feelings became lame,
You became depressed,
And others are to blame.
Happiness also disappeared
Your heart isn't the same
The fear you've feared
Is making your soul game.
Why did you do it Iceman?
Undo it if you can.

Is it a good bargain
For your emotional success?
You freeze anger and pain
And you feel less and less
You hide again and again
Your love 'n joy are a mess.
They joined the bandwagon
With your anger and fears.
Yes, alas, the deal is done
You suppress your fears,
Your love 'n joy are gone.

Iceman
How can I convince you
Warmth is the other direction?
Yes, It can melt you
Only to uncover faulty protection.
Iceman, whatever you do
Make peace with your affliction.
Want to be a real man?
Go for it while you can.

A Mama Bird's Nest

*"Unless the Lord builds the house, those who
build it labor in vain."*

(Psalms 127:1)

A Mama bird discovered a basket of plants hung on my patio
wall. Apparently, this basket had won accolade, and was
nominated to be the new home for Mama bird's new family.

We were watching the construction process straw by straw.
We witnessed the arrival of two tiny eggs in the basket, and our
hearts fluttered with joy when the two little chicks made their
first debut in our patio. We considered it an honor to have nature
share it's life with us on our premises.

We carefully checked on the little ones every now and then
when the mother was away. But one day we made a mistake
and touched the little chicks. Before we knew it, the nest had
been empty. Apparently, the Mama bird had smelled the odor
of a foreign creature in her babies skin and interpreted that to
be impending danger. We figured that she decided to move
because the neighborhood was hazardous for her babies' safety.
How she moved her chicks from the nest, remained a mystery.
All we know was that it was a courageous feat on the Mama
bird's part.

This bird exemplifies a responsible parent who is willing to do whatever it takes to protect her children. Sometimes we choose a certain spot in life for our children to live and participate in activities. We watch them being touched by the hands of the world, but do we give a hoot? We smell the odor of these foreign hands in the form of pride, lies, and loose morals. We watch them getting entangled into this predicament, but do we stop to untie the knots? In the end we may watch them engulfed in the ocean of worldly affairs seeking winning without fearing the Lord.

We may wonder: when did this entanglement take place? Why didn't I smell a rat from the beginning? How come I allowed my children to remain under these crummy circumstances?

The whys continue, and the regrets embark their shadow on our lives, and all becomes dim. I guess when we're too busy in our worldly affairs we lose our keen senses and don't see the impending danger. Raising children is not a part time job and removing them from a harmful environment is a continuous task. But the most important responsibility that lies upon our shoulders should be talking to them about God and His Salvation for us through Jesus Christ.

Your children can have all the trophies, medals, and awards they can acquire, but without the presence of God in their heart, they are at a loss. If we don't build our homes on the real **Rock, Jesus Christ,** then all our labor is in vain.

A Letter to Mom and Dad

I started an extremely good start
Because my parents were smart.
You sent me to the best schools ever
I gave it my best effort and endeavor.
I became an exceptional honor student,
With your **enthusiasm**, who wouldn't?

I want to tell you, Mom and Dad
You came to all my school events,
You were sure very proud and glad
To hear my teachers' compliments.

To every soccer 'n baseball game
You went 'n the picture was the same,
I can still envision your proud grin
Every time I made a goal to win,
Or when I happened to be the one
Who ran fast and made a home run.

A PTA meeting, you never missed,
You were on the **"Who's Who"** list,
You were well known 'n popular
Achieving various goals, so secular.

On the ocean of life, I was sailing
Smoothly in the **right** direction

Always going forward, but failing,
Was never the intended option.

When you were asked by a friend,
You didn't hesitate and you said
"All seems to be under control."
But you couldn't control my soul.

You see
My spirituality was compromised
'Cause talking about Jesus Christ
Was never a part of your plans
While you were busy with your clans.
My moral reasoning was twisted
I did not know God had existed.
I became a winner on my own merit,
I refused to give God any credit.

I developed an ego, so inflated
My conceit, I always updated,
My inner voice was so loud,
"You are trained to be proud!"
I always went for the highest score
And there was room for more,
I wanted to reach the highest sky,
And I felt this pressing urge inside
To leave the earth and get high
So, I went on a dangerous ride.
Drugs, was the actual trade name
Of this new exhilarating game.

You thought
That my upbringing was crystalline,
And that everything was going fine.
Until I dropped that big bomb
And you couldn't get it, Mom,
And you were shocked, Dad
I guess it was hard to understand
Because with everything I had,
I was supposed to be good not bad.

It was an unresolved quandary,
How I can tarnish your memory
Of a son with pristine reputation;
That was far from your expectation.

I know you were both disappointed
But it could have never been avoided.
You see, we were all deluded
When Jesus Christ was excluded.
How would you expect any success
When the heart is merely a mess?
Pride was suffocating my soul,
Sooner or later, I was bound to fall.

You thought you built my life on a rock,
But it crumbled because it was mock.
Too bad that in our daily parlance
The word "God" wasn't talked about
And because of this blatant avoidance,
We evidently paced the wrong route.

You certainly went by the book,
But, alas, it was not the right book
Christ wasn't Sovereign and Lord
You did not teach me His Word.

The Pagan Heart

*"She looks well to the ways of her household,
and does not eat the bread of idleness. Her
children rise up and call her blessed; her
husband also, and he praises her."*

(Proverbs 31:27,28)

Escaping the scorching sun of the Sahara Desert, the Ancient Egyptians lived by the undulating banks of the Nile River. The regularity of Nile floods, on which the economy of the entire country was based, was crucial. The Ancient Egyptians gave the Nile great importance that they did whatever it took to appease the gods so they would be in good terms with the natural force.

The most beautiful girl in the country was chosen to be the Nile's Bride. After going in a majestic procession in the Nile River, The bride was to be thrown into the river as a human sacrifice. It was considered a great honor to be chosen for that noble cause: the promotion of earth's fertility, self-preservation, and restoring the right relationship between man and the "sacred order." Who can argue with this noble cause? But does the end justify the means?

"Well, that is how the pagan mind worked back then. They

didn't really value human life!" You may think. But is the practice of human sacrifice exclusive to pagan cultures?

Every time we abandon our children for any reason, be it extra monetary gain, extra marital affairs, divorce, or negligence, we sacrifice them to our whims and desires. Working parents, and especially mothers, may argue, "It is for a noble cause. Life is hard and we have to make ends meet." Now mothers think that leaving their infant babies with babysitters and going to work is not a matter of choice anymore but an inevitability. It is true that stay-home moms are scrutinized in this modern world because in all sincerity many people fail to realize what it takes to run a healthy home. When running a company, its success is determined in terms of the monetary outcome. However, when running a household, the process may not lead to monetary outcome, but rather too many blessings that no one can measure by the worldly precepts.

So Moms, don't be threatened by the modern mentality. If your notion of staying home and caring for your children is not appreciated or understood, please know that you get your accolades from a higher power.

Be certain that what you're doing is much better than allowing your little ones to be thrown in the raging river of life fending for themselves away from the sanctity of the mother's loving heart.

Mom, You're Wasting Your Time

When we first got married,
You told me not to be worried
You explained from the start
You would work real hard.

When our first child came,
Things were not the same.
Your hard work was gone,
You left work for our son.
You don't help me anymore
And I don't know what for.

You want to be called
A homemaker or a mother.
Your career, you put on hold
And you don't even bother.

You left it up to me
To make ends meet.
You're no longer by my side
And you think I don't mind.
But while you're having fun
With your dearest little one,
While you're both playing
I will keep on saying,
Oh, my dear, sweet honey,

You don't bring in money
I truly have to confess
Your life is a real mess.
Hey, you'd better look!
You're wasting your time
That is, in my book,
The worst kind of crime.

Dichotomous Thinking

"For there is no distinction; since all have sinned and fall short of the glory of God, they are justified by His grace as a gift, through the redemption which is in Christ Jesus."

(Romans 3:22-24)

Dichotomous thinking is thinking in **black and white.** You see people as either good or bad, nothing in between. In other words, the gray color cannot be seen by your retina. You become very subjective in evaluating people's characters. You tend to go from one extreme to another because you cannot tolerate the inadequacies of people, especially your loved ones. According to you, they are either angels with halos, or horned devils.

As you fluctuate in your judgment from one extreme to another, your feelings also fluctuate from love to hate, and from hate to love, and so on. People who adopt this kind of thinking show ambivalence and confusion. If this distorted perception persists, maladaptive functioning occurs and stifles relationships.

The former kind of thinking negates the fact that we are all human beings with a combination of good and bad qualities.

First of all, we come to this world as sinners. Then, when we become believers in Christ, He gives us a new nature that resents sin. Nevertheless, this transformation does not make us angels. As believers we struggle on a daily basis and work with God so He can purify us and sanctify us. Does that mean we cannot fall? Of course not! But the difference is that in Christ, we develop a sensitive conscience that will rebuke us and make us approach God. Then, He will be always around to lend us His mighty hand to lift us and let us rise victoriously again.

I Am Not an Angel!

When we face any hardship
In what we call a relationship,
Communication comes to a halt
And you interpret it as my fault.
I, the woman whom you adore,
Stops wearing her halo anymore.
You see me as the devil incarnate,
All dressed in the color scarlet.

But
I am no angel and no devil,
I am neither black nor white.
I hope we reach that level
Of understanding that right.

When you're in an irrational episode
You hit me with a twisted moral code
That judges me to the core
And I don't fathom what for.
It seems to be very obvious
That you are very oblivious.

When we're not in complete accord,
Or our souls are not in alignment,
For you, it's the end of the world,
You freak out from bewilderment.

Perhaps it is your own mistake,
But that thought you can't entertain.
You put our well being at stake,
'Cause the guilt, you can't take.

When we're having a normal feud,
You turn on your oblivious mood.
To your heart,
Our love, you do not hold dear,
You switch gears from love to hate.
When you are in your loving gear,
Everything about me seems great.
And in your hateful gear, oh dear!
You tend to criticize and obliterate.

I am no angel and no devil
I'm neither black nor white
I hope we can reach that level
Of understanding that right.
I'm a human being, so normal,
Never claimed to be infallible.

I'm a combination of black and white
Yes, I do not always do things right,
But I can also be meek as a lamb,
So why can't you accept me as I am

Conditional Love

*"But God shows His love for us in that
while we were yet sinners Christ died for us."*
(Romans 5:8)

In my back yard, I had a yellow rosebush. I transplanted it in my front yard next to a red rosebush. When the buds blossomed, to my surprise, the rosebush produced pink roses instead of yellow roses. Because the yellow roses had interacted with the new environment, some changes took place.

People also interact with the environment and their behavior is apt to vary in different situations depending on their frame of mind at each particular moment. No one can ever react to two identical situations in duplicate. They may be cool, calm, and collected at one instant, and they can be seeing red at another depending on many factors. By the same token, no one can be "good" all the time. Even a "well-behaved" person can lose it somehow at least once in a blue moon.

To make your love for others contingent on their constant good behavior and perfection is far from being realistic. The two parties are bound to be disappointed. And whose moral code will you be setting, yours or theirs? Most people, including you and me, cannot adhere to anybody's code of perfection because sooner or later, our fallibility will be unraveled. Conditional love is a **lose-lose situation**. Your loved ones will beat their head off trying to adhere to your moral code for fear of losing you. If they fail, they'll face disappointment; and if they succeed, they may lose themselves in the process of trying to please and appease. The bottom line is that conditional love is unfair to your loved ones; besides, it sets you up for disappointments. Some people describe it as **"toxic love"** because it suffocates your loved ones, strips off their personality and freedom to express their love freely.

Intolerance, control, and lack of forgiveness are the trademarks of conditional love. "You do what I want, or else," are the famous words of someone who is not in the business of loving forever, but rather of someone who can easily withdraw his love whenever he pleases.

The forgiving and accepting nature of God's love for us, puts us all to shame. God loves us regardless of who we are and what we do. Yes, we are all sinners, and He is the Holy One. However, He loves us without any strings attached and He is sure after our salvation. God has no partiality, so who do we think we are to be picky in our loving style?

I Will Love You Forever, But

I want to live for the rest of my life
With you, my dearest lovely wife,
But if you defy me in any way,
I will not be compelled to stay.
You would be testing my reliability,
And it would be your responsibility.

You, I'll always love and cherish
My adoration will never perish
As long as you are good to me,
Of my love, you will be worthy.

You're so beautiful, my Love
This beauty is a gift from above.
This sure works to your advantage
As long as it doesn't fade away,
But if it tapers off with age,
I don't know what I'll do or say.
I cannot imagine your pretty face
Except glimmering with grace.

Forever, you will be
My bride 'n I your bridegroom
As long as, with me, you agree,
But you can be

The architect of your doom
If, eye to eye, we do not see.

You're my woman, I'm your man,
I will always be your greatest fan,
But once you start causing conflict,
I will give you my hardest verdict.

I assure you, as long as I have a lot
I will sure give you what I've got,
But if my earnings are meager,
To giving, I won't be that eager.

I will always be your best friend
If my rules you don't try to bend,
If you follow my direction,
And if in me, you entirely confide,
But if you cause any friction,
You will bring my hostile side.

I'll help you through thick and thin
As long as, to my wishes, you give in,
But if you become a detriment
To my well-being and welfare,
You will only get resentment
On that, we'll have to be square.

I will show goodness 'n kindness
If, your duties, you don't forsake,
But I'm not a paragon of forgiveness
When it comes to mistake after mistake.

And last but not least,
I don't like to be pushed to the max,
But my dearest beloved wife, relax
'Cause if you do everything you should,
I will be a husband, gentle and good.

Excuses, Excuses

"A man once gave a great banquet, and invited many; and at the time for the banquet he sent his servant to say to those who had been invited, "Come; for all is now ready. But they all alike began to make excuses."

(Luke 14:15-18)

- Why do you hate your neighbor?
- Because I envy him for what he has.
- Why do you like to bully people?
- Because I was abused.
- Why did you steal the money?
- Because I am poor.

When we have reprobate hearts, every bad deed comes with its explanation. Overuse of these explanations can lead to a pathology that we may call **pathological rendering of excuses** where no bad deed is given its real name, but rather attached to an excuse. Hatred would be justified because of envy, and stealing would be justified because of poverty, and so on. This pathology can persist to the extent that it may form weights on people's bodies and minds and make them too heavy and sluggish to go to the right direction towards the truth.

117

One of the symptoms of this pathology is the blindness of the heart, and in particular, selective blindness. This is the condition when we form a cloud of darkness to conceal our sin or what we don't want to see. The inability to see one's own sin makes everything seem OK while it is far from being OK.

When are we going to be in the clear? Only when we discard the excuses and start walking in the light of God. As long as God is extending His loving hand for us, and inviting us to walk in His path, we have no excuse to remain in our sinful condition. God is calling all for salvation, but alas, only a few respond to His invitation.

Guilty with Explanation

Your Honor,
Yes, I know I am guilty,
But guilty with explanation.
If you knew the reality,
You'd say it was temptation.
You are rich, and I am poor,
You don't know what I had to endure.
So, if I am somehow greedy,
It is because I was needy,
Grabbing was what I learned
When money was concerned.

Your life was certainly blessed
And everybody, you impressed.
Life gave you the best portion,
And I was left with misfortune.
So, if I'm a little depressed,
It is my misery expressed,
And if I am full of malice,
It is because I am jealous.

In your happy childhood,
You weren't necessarily good.
While I was the perfect child,
You were somehow wild,
Yet, you were having a blast

While I worked hard in my past.
So, if I act out of spite,
I consider it my right.

Adam,
We come to life with a bundle
That we must accept 'n well-handle.
Some are poor and some are rich,
Our bundles we cannot switch,
But we have a responsibility
To try to the best of our ability
To do our absolute best
"Blessed" or "not blessed."
We ought to show gratitude
Drop the complaint 'n the attitude.

So, poverty, you were given
You were supposed to
Accept it with thanksgiving
That is as opposed to
Spitefulness and bitter living.

So because of your conduct
You can get a harsh verdict.

But your Honor,
Don't treat me in this manner.
I was born with my sin
And, in me, it is inherent,
It seeps deep from within,
In my conduct, it's apparent.

Since the original fall
Man hasn't had any control
Over how he behaved,
To sin, he is enslaved.
So, if I can't be but reprobate,
Why would that make you irate?

My dear son Adam,
Why can't you fathom
You can't simply say,
Guilty with explanation
As long as there is a way
For your soul's salvation?

When Jesus Christ died
On the cross for you and me,
He was actually tried
For the sins of all humanity.
Charges against you were waved
This is how you could be saved,
He had to go through that ordeal
To offer you the deliverance deal.
He paid His life for your redemption
'N you hurt Him with your rejection.
But if you humbly repent and agree
To the deal, He can set your soul free.

So Adam, you have no excuse
There exists an open door
But to opening it, you refuse,
I don't understand what for.

You certainly have the key,
And I gave you the combination
"If God's son, you accept to be,
That will spell out your salvation."

PART TWO

The Everlasting Cycle of Truth

"If you continue in My word, you are truly My disciples, and you will know the truth, and the truth will make you free."
(John 8:31,32)

The Everlasting Cycle of Truth

"Worthy art Thou, our Lord and God, To receive
glory and honor and power, for Thou didst
create all things, "

(Revelation 4:11)

In searching for the truth, we may run in circles. One is a vicious cycle that leads to falsehood. The other one is a cycle of reaction that starts with God leading to the truth.

It is ironic how we human beings run in a vicious circle in our quest for the truth. Without God, we start our journey in life lacking any direction – only to stumble over the fallibility, limitation, and ignorance of our kind. We pursue our quest turning our backs against God, the only truth. Misled, we follow a mirage of imaginary truths – only to find ourselves in the scorching heat of the desert. Alone, tired, and disoriented, we go back to square one.

However, there could be another path to the truth. If we start our quest with a **contrite heart** approaching **God**, He will let the **Holy Spirit** work in us and reveal to us the truth. The truth is that Jesus Christ is the Son of God Who, with His act of salvation on the cross, we are granted salvation and eternal life. The more we live this truth, the easier we can develop a

spirit of discernment to choose **the truth**. Ultimately, we reside in **God's heart** and He lives in ours.

In the former vicious cycle, you are entrapped. Your only hope to get out is to look up in God's direction and allow Him to guide you. In the latter everlasting cycle of reaction, you start with God Who enfolds you with His tender loving care. Here, God's truth will be cultivated in your heart and it will become second nature to you to follow it.

In your search for the truth, focus on God, His attributes, and His kind encounters in your life. Then, give the glory to God.

Glory to God

I lift up my eyes
   to the sky above
From where I receive
   His heavenly love.
My help comes from the
   helpful mighty Lord
Who made heaven and
   earth by just a word.
He is our Shepherd
   we are His sheep.
How can He slumber
   or how can He sleep?
He is our potter
   we are the clay.
He won't forget we
   need His holy way.
In this dark world I
   live as a stranger,
God was estranged
   to live in a manger,
He was dethroned on earth,
   was humbly born
To lift my heart to
   His celestial throne.
Glory, glory to God
   in the highest.

He lifted the souls
 from the abyss.
In light, He dwells,
 has immortality,
He granted life
 to all humanity.
He stops the tempest
 and He calms the waves
From disturbance He
 delivers and saves.
He rebukes nature
 And He grants us peace,
Comforts the hearts by
 His surpassing grace.

In the Heavens
 Our father resides,
My heart belongs over there,
 in Him abides.
He dwells eternity,
 He is holy,
Yet, dwells He with
 the humble and lowly.

Will They Accept Me?

"See what love the Father has given us, that we
may be called children of God; and so we are."
(1 John 3:1)

The answer to three questions can coin your self-image: Who am I? What can I do? Will they accept me?

People struggle to prove themselves by creating an identity for themselves that fleshes out itself in conduct that reflects their capabilities. With their well-defined self-image and well-established capabilities, they seek acceptance: a reward that we all aspire. Often times, this is attained through a job or a career.

In Christ, our **identity** is well defined: **children of God**, and our **role** is engraved in stone: **loving and serving** others wherever we are. For example, in Christ, a mother would be God's child whose task is to love and serve her family whether this task is going to bring about lucrative reward or not. Money would not be the main concern. In Christ, the real reward is **doing God's will** to the best of our ability. It is true that a stay-home mom might not win accolades from the world that defines success in terms of the monetary compensation. However, the world is so narrow minded and short sighted. It cannot really estimate that the cost of raising unruly and ungodly children exceeds any amount of money a mother could earn from an "important" job.

Yes, everyone wants to feel important by holding that "important" job. But as mothers, we are more important to our children than we are to our boss. Being choosy in choosing a career is very crucial for experiencing healthy motherhood. Not falling in the trap of working more hours and more days for some extra dollars is a smart choice. All the money in the world cannot compensate for the moral loss of our children.

Imagine the cost of psychiatrists, jail cells, rehab centers, lawyers, or the entanglement in the court or social services system, not to mention the price of the moral damage, guilt, or regrets!

In Christ, a mother's job is clear: a loving, serving mother, and a teacher. Somebody has to teach children about the path of righteousness. If this topic is not covered, then all the mother's toil is in vain. Children need our undivided attention. If that means sacrificing a job, a career, or a sum of money at the end of every pay period, so be it. Whatever your situation is, whether you're a stay-home mom, or a working mom, don't forsake your role as a mother and teacher. No one can do it better than you. How you do it, is not important as long as you set your priorities straight, don't lose your true identity and role, and don't forsake your children. Don't be discouraged if you are not accepted by the world. May your heart be comforted when you know that God will definitely accept you as a mother and a teacher.

Who I Am

I'm not a physician,
I am not a lawyer,
I'm not a politician,
Not even a taxpayer.

I'm just the housewife,
And not the breadwinner.
I've lived my busy life
As a wife and caregiver.

I give more than I take,
But I love my job dearly.
I consider it no mistake
Serving others sincerely.

They often ask me and inquire
About my precious investment.
I report that I have no desire
But my family's contentment.

Being a mother and a wife,
I teach my children lessons
About life and eternal life,
About matters of essence.

About their inheritance

I say, for sure education,
Godly wisdom 'n intelligence
To pursue the route of salvation.

In my Heavenly Father, I trust,
My identity in Him is secure.
For that I am told I must
Know who I am for sure.

Yes,
My identity is well defined,
My mission is so refined.
I'm a teacher and a mother
One role enhances the other.

The Spiritual Invasion

"Therefore let no one pass judgment on you in question of food and drink or with regard to a festival or a new moon or Sabbath, these are only a shadow of what is to come; but the substance belongs to Christ.

(Colossians 2:16,17)

We've heard of political invasion when a country takes over another claiming territorial rights. But have you ever heard of **spiritual invasion** when someone invades your soul dictating to you how you should believe?

Nowadays the church suffers from the **"be like me"** syndrome. If you do not dress, talk, or behave like me exactly, then your faith should be questioned. Have you ever encountered people at your church who question your faith based on comparisons between life styles? If you don't fit their scope of expectation, they place you on the blacklist. How frustrating is that? How incomprehensible is it when human beings assume the role of God and give themselves the right to measure your faith and my faith using their fallible standards?

God is God of diversity. Imagine, no one on the face of this earth has the same fingerprints. Could that be a hint for us to respect our differences and work together as different pieces in the puzzle of life? Hopefully, when the picture is complete, it will represent our holy life as members of the one body of Jesus Christ.

Be Like Me

Don't you think it's a bit strange
That you would like me to change?
You want to loan me your **conviction**,
Imagining I did not have my own,
But pardon me you stand correction
'Cause mine I have not outgrown

You know, you've blatantly invaded
My inner affairs, heart, and soul
My personality, you have evaded
Don't want me to be "me" at all.

Can you hear my song?
Did you even try?
Is it loud and strong?
Or a soundless cry?

I am a person,
I have a soul,
I am an individual
Who wants to be whole.

I have integrity,
I am free,
Why don't you let me
Be what I'm fit to be?

If you want to see any change,
I can perform anything on stage
But my belief is completely off limit,
It's part of me, 'n I'm entitled to live it.
It's my possession, 'n mine to keep
Its living fruits are for me to reap.

Can you hear my song?
Why can't we agree?
Do you see what's wrong,
Or is it hard to see?

Don't you get it, or comprehend?
It's impossible for me to pretend.
If, to myself, I am not true,
Tell me, what will I be to you?
You think I'll gain your respect
If I fake it and play it as you direct?

Can you sing my song?
Do you feel the pain?
It is not too long
It is clear and plain.

I am a person,
I have a soul,
I am an individual
Who wants to be whole.

I have integrity,
I am free.

Why don't you let me
Be what I'm fit to be?

God's Voice Resonates Everywhere

*"And take the helmet of salvation, and the sword
of the Spirit, which is the word of God."*
(Ephesians 6:17)

To be alive is to have God's breath in us. To believe and
accept God's Son, Jesus Christ, is to have God's Spirit within
us. On this earth, we are not alone since we are connected to
God through the Holy Spirit. God sent Him to us to comfort,
instruct, and guide us in the way of righteousness. The Spirit of
God protects us with a sword, which is the word of God.

Without the presence of the Spirit of God we become
detached from the voice of God that speaks to us in myriad
ways. Believe me, the word of God is not rare in our days.
Even though we don't actually hear God's talking voice, He
talks to us through the Holy Spirit and, if we want, we can hear
his **word**, **voice**, **will**, or **instructions** in the Bible, in the
chirping of a bird, the trickling of water, a melodious song,
words of kindness, and even in the sound of roaring thunder.
Incidents and various events can also declare how great and
omnipotent He is.

So, if you seek to hear God's voice, don't go so far, just
open your ears and have your keen senses in the all set position

to hearken His word. Allow the Holy Spirit to sharpen your senses so you can interpret all stimuli and inputs from the world in the light of God's word.

So, "Today, when you hear His voice, do not harden your hearts as in rebellion." (Hebrews 3:15)

God Spoke to Me in a Hymn

I have always had assurance
Of God's salvation for me.
I've lived by divine providence,
As an heir of royalty.
I knew who my Father was,
I had amazing clarity.
People came with earthly laws
'N made me doubt this actuality.

They inspected my faith and deed
Using earthly ways and measures.
Who wouldn't fail to succeed
Faced by tests and pressures?

People really like to question
Your faith and who you are.
They do it with the intention
To show they're better, by far.

Even though they're more thunder
Than they are lightening
I gave in and knuckled under
A thought, that was frightening,
"What if my faith is not real?
And if so, what will be the deal?"

Because of their rejection,
For a while, I had no direction.
I kept on asking, "Who am I?"
And I did not fail to cry.

It was an episode that pierced
My spiritual armor badly,
My joy and peace had ceased
And I carried on so sadly.

I went to the Bible study,
My wounded heart was ready
To listen attentively and to learn
To God, I presented my concern.
I lifted my weeping heart to Him,
And He spoke to me in a hymn,
"I felt every tear drop when
In darkness you cried
And I strove to remind you
That for those tears I died."

To me it was like a miracle
A dialogue with God, a response?
That was absolutely incredible
God came to my defense.

The more I felt really terrible,
The more His voice became audible.
His message was loud and strong
He reminded me to whom I belonged
I did not have to wait for long,
He spoke to me in His song

He proclaimed to me His grace,
And assured me of my faith.

Should I Change the Color of My Skin to Please You?

"So we speak, not to please men,
but to please God Who tests our hearts."
(1 Thessalonians 2:4)

Observing nature, we find out that animals have different tactics that they use to help them cope with the environment. To protect themselves, chameleons change their skin color very fast to be camouflaged with the surrounding. This way their predator won't see them.

There is a saying that says, "When you are in Rome, do as the Romans do." This is true when it comes to observing special traditions and aspects of the culture. Out of respect, we should honor the different customs of different groups of people as long as we don't jeopardize our beliefs.

On the other hand, when it comes to your beliefs and convictions, no one has the right to ask you to change them for anybody's sake. These convictions are yours and they comprise your entity. To compromise them to please others, would mean losing yourself. Contrary to some creatures in nature, human beings have one color of skin. They can't change it to match whatever situation they're in.

When we are in Christ, we are bathed in His forgiveness and our color should reflect the purity of our new creation in Christ. That is actually the only color we should reflect. We owe Christ this much.

Living in this confusing world with different demanding people, we tend to change our color to suit their demands. In the process, we can lose our pure color. But is it worth the trouble?

What Do I Want to Prove?

In people's shadow, I've lived my life
Trying to impress and to please,
I've wasted my whole life's strife
Not to edify myself, but to appease.

I utilized all tactics and whatever
To win their undivided attention.
So I focused all my endeavor
On passing their harsh inspection
Which I honestly could have never
Passed in any state or dimension.

I used to wear a phony disguise
To communicate I was their ally,
It took me a while to realize
I was paying a price, so high
Just to be the apple of their eye.
It was an off the wall scheme
To realize an unattainable dream.

The more I strove to prove
That I deserved their admiration,
The more I did inadvertently disprove
That I'd amount to their expectation.

147

I didn't improve or ameliorate
My life's status or quality
And by that I did instigate
A compromise on my integrity.
I delved into the wrong path
I realized that in the aftermath.

Now,
I'd like to make a plea bargain,
Destroy the façade, set myself free,
Live a life, so true and genuine,
And strive to be the real "Me."

God Is Forever Faithful

"The steadfast love of the Lord never ceases,
His mercies never come to an end; they are new
every morning, great is Thy faithfulness."

(Lamentations 3:22, 23)

Light is forever present wherever the sun is. With the presence of the light, darkness has no entity or power because it is simply the absence of light. God is the light of the world, so, no darkness can overtake us as long as we reside in God's heart and He resides in ours.

God grants us to reflect His light in our homes, at work, and with friends and enemies. If the source of our light is God, then, shouldn't we, at least, reflect a portion of His attributes? Faithfulness is one attribute of God that assures us of His love, forgiveness, care, protection, and stability. Imagine if we can reflect just one portion of God's faithfulness! Wouldn't life be different for those who encounter us?

Faithfulness is like a **guarantee** that no matter what, we will be dependable, reliable, and consistent under any given condition. Trials and tribulations may hit and the carnal hearts may change, but the spiritual hearts will remain the same, unaltered, and undefiled by the tumult and uncertainty of the world. Life or people may turn against us, but if we hold onto our position in God's heart and remain faithful, our light may overtake the darkness around us.

So let us discard our judgmental hearts and put on our faithful ones. May our sincerity enlighten the hearts of the people around us!

Declaration of Faithfulness

I promised you to love and cherish
You till death do us part,
And I really meant every word
From the bottom of my heart.
I will always keep my promises,
I will never leave your premises
Because
Faithful and loving, that is me,
That is exactly what I want to be.

In sickness and in health,
In bad times and in wealth,
Handsome or not,
You're all I've got.
Young or even very old,
My heart, on you, is sold.
I love you in any condition,
As you are, I like this rendition.

Nothing will weaken our unity
Wars, trials, or even calamity
For the love 'n unity we're given
God has engraved in heaven.
We are one; we're no longer two,
You're part of me, I'm part of you.

You can be hurtful or unjust,
You can be intolerable, but
I will never retaliate,
I'll forgive 'n tolerate
Because I believe nothing is incurable
And that my undying love is capable
Of healing my marital anomalies
'N bring out your redeeming qualities.

To your mistakes, I will be blind,
The goodness in you, I will find.
I will follow God's love to the letter,
I will sacrifice to make you better
Because
Faithful and loving, that is me,
That is exactly what I want to be.

It Is Unfair, but ...

*"By the great mercy we have been born anew
to a living hope through the resurrection of Jesus
Christ from the dead, and to an inheritance
which is imperishable, undefiled, and unfading,
kept in heaven for you."*

(1 Peter 1:3,4)

I have encountered a lady who had an illegal status in the United States. Without a job, she lived with her boyfriend without the sanctity of marriage. Somehow she managed to receive child support and food stamps for her children whom she had from different fathers in the U.S. Even though her boyfriend was able to work, he was still taking disability money from the government. I was informed that the lady did not want to either work or marry her boyfriend lest she should lose the child support she was receiving.

I looked at her situation and I couldn't help but compare her life with mine. This lady had an illegal status in the country and, of course, she didn't contribute to the country by either working or paying taxes. She adamantly chose to manipulate the system by having babies illegitimately from different men. She actually chose a family structure that was not acceptable by most standards. Yet, this lady managed to get money, food stamps, and even free medical and psychological care provided by some nonprofit organizations.

On the other hand, I am a citizen of the U.S. I chose to get married and have legitimate children. My husband and I work very hard and, certainly, we pay taxes. Nevertheless, I have never received any benefits or extra money when I had my children. We pay for our healthcare and if we were to seek psychological help, we would have to pay a fortune.

Again, I looked at my situation and I couldn't help but feel sorry for myself. It seems that we get penalized for being honest and honorable citizens. It looks to me that people who don't go by the book get more attention and benefits. I prayed about how I felt and God let me understand the crux of the matter. Even though I pay to the government more than I receive benefits, I should be thankful for the fact that I belonged to my country and didn't have to lie, cheat, and manipulate to get by.

By the same token, we encounter, unfairness in our interaction with friends and family. We feel hurt because we expect a better treatment from those who are supposed to love us the most. However, when I pray about this matter, I come to the same conclusion. Whatever unfairness I face in this world, I should be thankful that I am God's child and I belong to a heavenly kingdom where I don't need to play games or take advantage of others to feel gratified. I am certain I am accepted, loved, and cherished by the most loving Father and King.

So, if this worldly kingdom is unfair, I will not change my convictions to join the bandwagon of manipulators. I wouldn't need that because I have a **heritage** in the **kingdom of heaven** that exceeds all the benefits I could have taken on earth.

My Love Will Always Abound
Even If You Don't Come Around

When you hurt me my dear friend,
Forgiving you has become my trend.
I vowed not to ever condescend,
'N to understand you until the end.

A trend of kindness and empathy,
I have never regretted I started,
But you showed me no sympathy
'N more hurt, you launched 'n darted.
I did my best to deter your apathy
And you took my tolerance for granted.

The more your unknown inclination,
I intentionally kept on defending,
The more you found an invitation
To become more heartrending.

At all times I try to the best of my ability
To allow our souls to be in alignment,
But you cannot comprehend the reality
That I'm fulfilling God's assignment.

So, go ahead and, my character, degrade,
My heart won't turn bitter or sour

'Cause in whatever I do, I win accolade
Not from you, but from a higher power.

God taught me His kindheartedness
When He showed me love 'n forgiveness
It's an attribute engraved on my soul
No one, even you, can suppress at all.
It's a reflection of God's faithfulness
That the world failed to show you.
You thought it was my weakness
That you had the urge to subdue,
So, you held on to your ruthlessness
And the hurt, you couldn't undo.

To your alleged, so-called strength.
You make a point to pay homage,
You don't realize to what length
You lack audacity and courage.
Courage, my dear friend
Is not for the one scared to mend,
Or for the one who pretends,
It's for those who make amends.

So, my friend, keep on demoralizing
And I will keep on emphasizing
My love will always abound,
Even if you didn't come around.

The Art of Giving

"For God loves a cheerful giver."
(2 Corinthians 9:7)

The more seeds you plant, the more flowers you'll see in your garden. The more money you invest, the more profit you'll get. The more love, care, and compassion you demonstrate, the better human being you'll become and the better world you'll generate.

The results of the equation for **giving,** is kind of different. You subtract from what you have, but you have more in the end. In order to see the profit, you have to put on different kinds of eyeglasses, the kind that is made to particularly see the will of God.

The will of God for us is to give profusely without thinking about the outcome and without expecting a reward in return. Whether we get a reward in the form of money or gratitude and whether we get an intrinsic reward or not, that should not be our motivation for giving. When living with God, just the act of giving would produce peace and joy: in other words, intrinsic satisfaction.

So, keep on giving from an undefiled heart and watch your heart grow and yield the **fruit of the Spirit** in abundance: love, joy, peace, patience, kindness, goodness, faithfulness, gentleness, and self-control.

Giving is like planting seeds, the more seeds you plant, the more crop you'll reap in your heart.

> *"And whoever gives to one of those little ones even a cup of cold water because he is a disciple, truly, I say to you he shall not lose his reward."*
> (Matthew 10:42)

What You Give Does Multiply
What You Retain, Can't Edify

Through life, we are faced
With losses and many regrets.
Our **good deeds** go to waste,
And even the best of our intents.

One good deed over here,
And another over there,
Kindness, you really endear,
You like to plant everywhere.

But kindness, your friends,
Do not give you back,
Its giving flow ends
When it's on the other bank.

It disappears in thin air
As if it had never been granted.
You think it isn't fair
Not to reap what you've planted.

You review in your head
What has been said,
"Life takes but never gives,
Condemns 'n never forgives."

We **work hard** to attain
A higher level or merit,
But our work goes in vain,
What we build, we don't inherit.

But if you observe diligently
God's work 'n listen attentively,
You will feel His abundant blessing,
You won't notice what you're missing.

When you experience God's grace,
The unkindness that you face,
May as well seem insignificant
Because what is really important
Is God's mercy 'n forgiveness,
His tender heart 'n acceptance.

When kindness, you plant,
You reap it in your heart
While your friend's hardness can't
Bring peace, or make them smart.

For what you give does multiply,
And produce fruit of the Spirit.
What you retain cannot edify,
Won't help you attain any credit.

So,
In order to show your intelligence,
You have to give with abundance.
You will get your timely reward

Here on earth, or in Heaven above:
God's approval, not man's regard,
And a giving heart full of love.

Keep on giving and know
This is the right way to grow.
Because the fine art of giving
Reveals the secret of living.

And when you give, be careful
To give but what is beautiful.
Learn not to complain 'n never
Be but a content, cheerful giver.

For what you give does multiply,
But what you retain won't edify.

Your Better Half

"What therefore God has joined together,
let not man put asunder."

(Matthew 19:6)

At the time of the Puritans it was said that the soul and body made up a person. The spiritual part was given more caliber so the soul was called **"the better half."**

In the sixteenth century the English author, Sir Philip Sidney applied the term to refer to the matrimonial union so either the husband or the wife would refer to the other partner as "the better half" indicating a 50/50 partnership.

"My better half," what a wonderful way of addressing your sole partner? And if the relationship between body and soul corresponds to the relationship between a husband and wife, then one will assume that the two are inseparable. If each partner joins the other with the understanding that the other partner comprises 50 percent of himself/herself, then there will be a revolutionary attitude when conflict arises. Each one will be concerned with appeasing the other partner so there wouldn't be any schism in the structure: body and soul. **There will be one option: maintaining harmony rather than separation.**

The Bible talks about this matrimonial union, "Therefore a man leaves his father and his mother and cleaves to his wife, and they become one flesh." (Genesis 2:24)

So, **"my better half"** I think I should treat you as I treat myself. You should be tolerated, forgiven, loved, cherished, and exalted.

How Can I Leave You?

To My Partner, My Dearest Dear:
I wish to be honest and sincere.
At one weak moment of doubt
I cried my weary heart out,
Our problems, I couldn't ignore,
And I couldn't take it anymore.
Many solutions; I had sought
In distress, I pondered a thought,
"For the time you had it your way,
For playing all games under the sun,
For all the words you didn't say,
For noble deeds that weren't done,
For all the guilt, on me, you lay,
I'll pack my bags and I'll be gone!"

I was certain it was my only choice,
And I kept on hearing this voice,
"For all the times you didn't care,
For promises you chose to break,
For all the laughs you refused to share
For the closeness you couldn't take,
For all put downs that weren't fair,
I'm leaving you 'n it's your mistake!"

But
How can I have the heart to depart

And leave you, my precious friend?
Your faults shouldn't set us apart,
I will stick by you until the end.

How can I leave my sole mate,
My matrimonial duties, neglect?
I intend to love you at any rate,
My wedding vows, I won't forget.
I should learn how to tolerate,
To cherish, to love, 'n to respect.
What God joins in His name
No one has the right to put asunder.
Who am I to judge and blame?
My real job is to surrender,
To exalt you, and to give,
To support, and to forgive
No matter good or bad you do
I must remember my sins, too.

How can I leave my helper
Whom God, for me, has assigned
To be my crown and my scepter?
That is how you were designed.

**No, I won't leave you ever
I'll stick by your side forever.**

Opening the Line of Communication

*"For He has made known to us in all wisdom
and insight the mystery of His will, according
to His purpose which He set forth in Christ as a
plan for the fullness of time, to unite all things
in Him, things in heaven and things on earth."*
(Ephesians 1:9,10)

To grow to your full potential is to have integrity, to become whole. A human being is made out of soul, mind, heart, and body. The mind has the capacity to orchestrate the whole gamut of emotions and body conduct. You can become the master of your mind by choice. What guarantees you're making the right choice is the message you receive from God.

If you need an agent that can keep the line of communication between you and God open, consult your soul. Your soul is the liaison between you and God. It yearns to be with its Creator and can relay heavenly messages to you. Because we have a soul, we are able to feel the presence and hear the voice of God through the Holy Spirit. The most important thing is to have your soul in alignment with the will of God.

Jesus Christ coming to earth opened the line of communication between us and God. By accepting His act of salvation on the cross, we proclaim our alliance to God; hence, He calls us His children. When Jesus Christ resurrected from the dead and ascended to heaven, the line of communication was not cut because He sent us His Holy Spirit. In Jesus Christ, our souls are in unity with God our Father.

The soul is the moral and spiritual force behind your mind. It helps the mind with its decisions. The mind, in turn, is the force behind your feelings and behavior. Of course you want your mind to be a benign and functional force in your life. This condition is contingent upon the nature of communication you have between your soul and God. If the line of communication is open and clear, then you've attained harmony between the four forces in you: mind, emotions, body, and soul. Now you've chosen to listen to the voice of God and you're on your way to reaching your ultimate goal: integrity.

My Integral Birth

Integrity was my ultimate goal
I truly wished to become whole
Mind, heart, body, and soul
I asked,
"Could that be attainable at all?"

I have always had good intentions
To follow God's exact directions,
I did the best I could
To be the way I should.
As hard as I tried, I failed
Because I was being assailed;
My desires were in big dissonance
With the wishes of my conscience.
I thought I could be kind of clever
If I tried to triple my endeavor,
The outcome was just the same,
And I didn't know who to blame.

It seemed that my nature, so sinful
Was not in any way being helpful.
It made
My mind, heart, body, and soul
Each assume a conflicting role.

But

When I dared to open my heart
To listen to God's redeeming word,
I made a pledge for a new start
To live for Jesus Christ, my Lord.

My **heart** was taken care of
When I did not turn it off.
In Jesus Christ I could find
Forgiveness and peace of **mind.**
To my soul, my **body** connected,
And by God, it was directed.
My **soul** became the liaison
Between God and sinful me.
This way I could carry on
God's eternal plan for me.

Jesus Christ
Opened the line of communication
When He offered reconciliation.
Through Christ's act of salvation,
We were granted the unification
Between God in heaven, and earth
Which facilitated my integral birth.

In Jesus Christ I can attain integrity
From now and on until eternity
Through the healing He has brought
For my body, soul, heart, 'n thought.

There is really nothing greater
Than being united with the Creator

God's Delegation

"I planted, Apolos watered, but God gave the growth."

(1 Corinthians 3:6)

In God's vineyard, we are called to serve the Lord. The harvest is plentiful, but the laborers are few. God entrusts us to plant and water the seeds while He orchestrates the whole process of growth. It is God's miraculous touch that enables anyone to believe and to grow in faith.

God's grand plan is for everyone to know Him and live for Him. He starts by delegating to you and me the responsibility to reach out and spread the Gospel of truth. Our job is to relay the message from God. However, sometimes we get the feeling that we are very important to the extent that we give ourselves credit for winning people to Christ. Actually, it is God's work through the Holy Spirit that enables us to believe and to live up to our faith.

In serving the Lord we have to work in humility and realize that we're not doing God a favor, but rather by obeying Him we receive numerous blessings. When God calls us to serve, He does that for our own good because witnessing for Him allows us to draw near God and that is His ultimate purpose for us. So no one has the right to be boastful when there is fruit because it is actually God's doing and calling.

Who Is Planting the Seed?

My life flashed before my eyes,
I felt regrets and I asked whys.
I thought I have planted a tree,
But living fruits, I did not see.

With care, I watered the soil,
Love, was the secret of my toil,
But, fruits, it did not bear
Despite all the love and care.

In the Bible, God spoke to me,
"I can see you planted the seed,
And you watered the plant indeed.
Know, your toil won't be in vain,
But "growth" is out of your domain.
As long as, your effort, you invest,
For sure there will be a harvest.
You'll be awarded for your job
Whether or not you see the crop.
Please, leave the growth to Me
And fruit will come eventually!
Just keep on planting the seed
And help My mission succeed."

What I understood in essence
Was to discard the arrogance,

Do my job with modest humility,
'N give God His rightful authority.

God is asking you and me,
"Who, my flock, will feed?"
And it's our responsibility
To demonstrate a good deed.

There sure will be a fruit
Whether scarce and destitute,
Whether visible or invisible,
It is actually God's miracle.
God is the exclusive Creator
Of any newly born heart.
Believe that sooner or later
Living fruits, He will impart.

So, the real question now
Is not "When?" or "How?"
It's "Who's planting the seed
So God's mission will succeed?
Who, His flock, will feed?
Who's demonstrating a good deed?
Who's meeting this pressing need,
And lovingly planting a seed?"

Approaching God

"But God Who is rich in mercy, out of the great love with which He loved us, even when we were dead through our trespasses, made us alive together with Christ (by grace you have been saved)"

(Ephesians 2:4,5)

Some people are afraid to approach God because they think He is going to withhold His salvation until He examines their past sins, weighs them, and then gives them a grade on a curve; and based on that they can be eligible or not to receive His grace. They compare themselves to others and thus, score very low in the field of righteousness.

However, God's grading system to pass the course of eligibility to receive grace and salvation is based on credit/no credit system. The most important qualification we need on our resume is a heart open to receive God's salvation. Remember the thief on the right-hand side of Jesus on the cross, he had no qualifications whatsoever, but he had a repentant heart that was open for forgiveness and was longing to be with God.

So, if your sinful life is standing in your way of drawing

near God, take it with you and cast it at the foot of the cross. If you are heavy laden with your guilt, repent and God will issue you the ticket to freedom in His Son Jesus Christ.

Just don't focus on your sin, focus on God's forgiveness, and move forward towards a righteous life to work out your salvation with fear and trembling.

Bathed in the Ocean of Forgiveness

They asked, "How are you today?"
And that is what I used to say,
"I am just hanging in there,
I am just grasping at straws
I carry my wound everywhere,
And a life full of my own flaws.

"The second half of my life, I'll spend
Trying to fix my life and mend
Getting rid of the riffraff
I brought in the first half.

"Whenever I attempt to cry
My tear ducts become dry
But I start to cry from within
Regretting my nagging past sin
I manage to shed one teardrop
That makes the time stop
It takes me to my sinful years
When I lived in my fears
It stirs up much emotion
It fills my heart like an ocean.

"I live in an emotional avalanche
Tormented and torn from inside.
My mistakes, I wish to launch

On a never-to-come-back ride."

Then I spoke with my physician
On how to get rid of my fear.
He said, "I am not a magician
Who can make it disappear."
Anyway, a prescription, he wrote
And assured, "It's a good antidote
To ward off fears, guilt and shame,
Take it, and you won't be the same
It is made out of God's kindness.
Grace 'n mercy are the ingredients
Of this miraculous medicine.
These are the right doze and contents
To counter effect your past sin."

At the foot of the cross, I went
To God, I relinquished control
He gave me faith 'n I did repent
So, He redeemed and saved my soul.

Then I shed one teardrop
That made my time stop,
But I realized this time
The extent of my crime
Compared to how God is merciful
And how His love is bountiful.
Now,
In God, I am a new creation,
And my old life has passed.
I am in the era of salvation
My burden is lifted at last.

Now,
They ask, "How have you been?"
I say, "I am free of my sin
God will not let it overcome,
He'll remind me of who I've become:
I'm His child who was bathed
In the ocean of His forgiveness,
And when the question is raised
I say,
"It's not me, but His faithfulness."

The Worried Heart

"Have no anxiety about anything, but in everything by prayer and supplication with thanksgiving let your request be known to God. And the peace of God, which passes all understanding, will keep your hearts and your minds in Christ Jesus."

(Philippians 4:6,7)

People who worry too much have a problematic attitude towards **trust issues.** Trusting people, life, and even themselves becomes a difficult task. Their judgment relies on their **fear** and their limited **negative experiences** in life. Worriers become pessimists and their pessimism and negative thoughts act like chokers that hinder their progress in life.

Notice that the origin of the word "to worry" in Greek means "to choke" or "to strangle." Worry has the ability to debilitate us and smother our peace. Orchestrated by fear, worry colors our life in dark dim colors making us expect the worst.

God commands us not to worry and not to fear anything in life because He promises to be with us. Psalm 23 expresses the heart of someone who is completely in the presence of the Lord and who is dependent on Him, "Even though I walk in the

179

valley of the shadow of death, I fear no evil; for Thou art with me; Thy rod and Thy staff, they comfort me." (Psalms 23:4) The psalm reflects David's strong faith in God and his assurance that God is his **Protector**.

We cannot have David's assurance without entering into a relationship with Jesus Christ and experiencing His faithfulness. In Jesus Christ, the Holy Spirit becomes our **Comforter**, and trusting in Him liberates us from fear. As if we were children counting on the strength of our parents, we would become adults counting on our almighty and omnipotent Father Who does not slumber. When we focus our attention on Jesus Christ, our outlook on life becomes bright and our prognosis in each situation becomes good.

For example, to someone who worries, any drawback in his plans is considered the end to his strife in attaining his goal. On the other hand, the same drawback for someone who holds onto the Lord triggers enthusiasm that enables him to triple his endeavor to reach the desired goal.

Our trust in God leads us to surrender to the will of God. From surrender, we extract contentment and thanksgiving. When we put tomorrow in God's hands, today becomes much lighter, more tolerable, and full of hope.

Carried on the Wings of Love

To My Daughter,
To the most precious of all
Part of my body and soul,
When you fell sick and helpless,
My heart grew weary 'n restless.
I spent a sleepless night after night
Pondering how I could do it right.

I did not quite know what to do
Your illness gave us such a scare,
I wanted to lovingly give to you
The best tender loving care.

My worn out heart was troubled,
And through my life, I muddled.
I worried each hour and each day
I had no other choice but to pray.
God gave me peace and patience,
And I had an epiphanic experience.

God looked upon me from the sky
With caring heart, He heard me cry,

Amidst all the scary mayhem
I was touched by an amazing touch,
Worry was out of my system,
God proved He loved us so much.
My burden, heavy as a boulder
Was gently lifted off my shoulder.

I was held on God's caring hand
Lifted above all the worries I had,
Was carried on the wings of love,
And granted peace from above.

On the Lord, I learned to depend,
For you 'n me, I didn't need to fend.
I learned to yield and surrender
'Cause I have the greatest Defender.

Through the whole sickness ordeal,
God was always there ready to heal.
Through it all we were made aware
An assigned guardian angel was there.

Two years later we were assured,
Your body was completely cured,
However, the healing of our soul
Was the most miraculous of all.

Only If …

*"And which of you by being anxious
can add one cubit to his span of life?"*
(Matthew 6:27)

"If I could manipulate people and situations around me, the world would be a safer place for me.

"If I twist facts and lie about certain incidents, I can fool people to think that I am a good person and I have better control over my life.

"If I can manipulate, lie, twist the truth, and play games, I will place people where I really want them to be; below me and I'm above them."

Have you ever encountered this logic of someone who claims absolute control? Most probably. Yes, it is scary not to be in control of our lives, but what's scarier is to hand the rudder of control to a fallible human being even if it were myself. With an ignorant captain, the ship can go in the wrong direction, get lost, or drown.

The stormy winds of life hit us from time to time. Anxious about their safety, some people duck or hide. Others assume control and use all their worldly devices such as lies and games.

They can claim victory for a while until a mightier tempest hit and then they find out how powerless they are.

On the other hand, children of God neither hide, nor take matters into one's own hands; they surrender their ship to God Who is the best navigator. Not only is He the best captain, but also the One Who formed the sea and earth. Who else would have greater knowledge of **our life's map?**

So, if lies, games, and manipulations had been your worldly tactics and weapons to ward off the darts of this unfriendly world, discard them. Just allow Jesus Christ our Lord to handle the steering wheel of your life guiding you in the right path according to His grand scheme.

I Used to Be in Control

I did not believe in fate
So, in order to be in control,
I used to lie and manipulate,
In fact, I did not care at all
If I made people sad or irate.

To put people where I wanted,
I played all games under the sun.
All cunning skills I darted,
I thought it was sort of fun
To outsmart the simple 'n naïve
And, my fibs, make them believe.
It was ingenious inspiration
To play them as pieces of chess.
My tactics and manipulation,
They could never guess.

In the middle of my tricks,
I heard news I couldn't fix,
"I don't know what to say,
Your wife has passed away.
She was in her house alone
When God chose to take'er home."

I could not believe my ears
She was young, she wasn't ill.

This epitomized my fears,
It happened against my "will."
It happened without my permission,
It happened out of the blue.
Is it time for real submission,
A concept, I can't construe?

Does that mean that destiny,
A word, not in my diction,
Can hit me fast 'n suddenly
Without any guess or prediction?
Maybe that really means
I am not in charge anymore.
Then what were those schemes
Planned and used for?

God answered me,
"I really want you to know
It was time for your wife to go.
Your services were not needed
Anyway,
They couldn't have succeeded.
It's time for you to know,
Of your control, you must let go,
I am in charge of the universe
So step aside, and let Me be,
Your lies, I will not endorse,
With your schemes, I won't agree.
So step aside and surrender,
Allow Me to be your defender."

I realized that all my games

Could not save her life.
With all my victory claims,
I couldn't claim back my wife.

You Brought Us to Our Knees

"We know that in everything God works for good with those who love Him, who are called ccording to His purpose."

(Romans 8:28)

Think of all the times you felt vulnerable and sought help. Was it when you had a problem, when you were sick, or when you encountered death occurring to your friends, family, or even strangers? Can you remember what was going on, on your mind or how you felt in your heart?

In the face of adversities, we can't help but feel and think that we are helpless and vulnerable. The definition of the word "vulnerable" is "being susceptible to attack or damage." Vulnerability also represents a state of being not in control experiencing inner discord.

Often times, this inward dissonance cannot be harmonized by outward worldly solutions, but rather by the help of a higher power from above. In times of need or loss of control, we find ourselves willingly wanting to regain control by relinquishing control to God. What an amazing sight when we present our white flag proclaiming our acceptance of God's sovereignty over our lives! Would that be considered defeat or victory?

188

On September 11, 2001, the enemy expressed their hatred and launched a spiteful attack on us as a nation and on humanity in general. We were astounded because, in a way, we thought we were invincible as a nation. However, losing control in such a manner awakened our hearts to the reality of our vulnerability. It was a horrible ordeal, but amidst the dust and rubble existed the key to real victory: going back to our roots and establishing a relationship with God; it was about time. Amidst this **manmade evil** and on ground zero, our hearts were humbled and we were brought to our knees. Yes, we remembered what prayer was all about: a communion between a **vulnerable human being** and an **omnipotent God** who wants to restore peace and accord in the humans' hearts.

189

Do I Know You?

Do I know you my fellow human being?
Have we ever met at any time before?
I know we are not exactly agreeing,
But what's your outrageous rage for?

I'm asking you for what reason 'n why
You wanted my friends to die!
Do we know each other at all?
To whom did you sell your soul?

At what point in time, our relationship
Developed to become that sour?
Couldn't you just have a grip
Instead of using your evil power?

Do you know how much trouble
You had caused and inflicted?
People were buried under rubble,
In just a moment, not predicted.
What message did you want to send
That, my friends' life, you wanted to end?

You inflicted harm on my sisters and brothers,
You didn't stick around and chose to die.
Had you lived 'n seen the pain of others,
Would you have had the tears to cry?
To humanity, you are a traitor

How do you think you'll meet your creator?

You didn't live to see the flames,
You didn't live to see the smoke.
While playing your sick games,
The outcome was not a joke.

You broke the bond of humanity
At a hasty moment of insanity.
You turned brothers against brothers
You didn't give a hoot about others.

And I still have this question:
Have you ever seen my face
Before you died in your destruction
And my life, you chose to deface?
Did we engage in a conversation
That triggered your indignation?
Why, suddenly, and out of the blue,
In flames, am I introduced to you?

Why on earth did you do it?
Did you want to break our spirit?
You wanted to bring us to our knees
And yes, you have succeeded.
Now everybody sees and agrees
That this is what we really needed.

You thought you will break us apart,
But we became a united nation.
The tragedy empowered us to start
A life of prayer and supplication.

Just a Grain of Sand

*"Blessed is the man who endures trials,
for when he has stood the test he will receive
the crown of life which God has promised to
those who love Him."*

(James 1:12)

Just a grain of sand in the ocean can do wonders. It can by chance enter an oyster, spend a number of nights there, and then leave in a royal gown when it turns into a pearl.

When the grain enters the body of the oyster, it is like a foreign body that irritates and hurts the oyster. So to protect itself, the oyster produces a pearly layer to cover the cause of the pain. Think about it for a moment, that pearl starts as an irritation and then it becomes this magnificent piece of jewelry.

Have you ever experienced that in your life? An annoying grain of sand that forces its way into your life and causes trouble. When that happens to you, don't be discouraged. **Just anticipate the birth of a pearl.**

The element of contrast is very important in life. If you are painting a picture, the presence of yellow, for example, enhances the green. Outlining a white area with black makes it more visible. The fact that there is night, makes us appreciate the presence of the sun. The fact that there are valleys, makes us aspire to climb mountains. We particularly appreciate the calm after a storm, peace after periods of war. The same rule applies when we're talking about the difficulties in our life. Problems have the power to instigate prayers and a hope for a better tomorrow. If each day brought nothing but success, life would be unexciting. Why dream or hope for anything, if all is available?

When we face difficulties we tend to analyze life in light of hardships and adversities, and we see one color: black, nothing else. But if we widen our scope, we will be able to see the light at the end of the tunnel and the lining underneath the clouds. The feeling of contentment can be enhanced because of the difficulties we encounter. It is not easy, but sometimes failing is crucial, so success wouldn't be taken for granted. And sometimes things have to be difficult before getting easy. **Again, we need the element of contrast in our life.**

Life teaches us that like the oyster, we are equipped to produce a pearly layer to deter the effect of our problems. Problems, difficulties, and trials can irritate us any way they want. But be certain they are there for a reason. All it takes is patience. **If we accepted them and embraced them, in the end we could discover a pearl within our hearts.**

The Birth of a Pearl

It goes with the motion
Of the ripples of the ocean.
This minute grain of sand,
Not knowing where to land,
Looks for a safe place to hide
Then finds its way inside
A far from helpless oyster.
The purpose is not to pester,
But eventually it irritates
So, the hurt oyster filtrates
A pearly layer of protection
To cover the cause of infliction.

This little wandering grain
Is no longer anything plain,
With the help of the oyster
It gets a new pearly texture,
The grain of sand is adorned
When a **pearl** is formed.

It starts as an irritation,
But given time and patience
It will earn your admiration
And you'll value its elegance.

Like this grain of sand,
Troubles find their way
To our life 'n decide to land,
But what can we possibly say,
We ought to understand
Troubles hit and usually stay.

But just wait a minute!
I have the Holy Spirit!
Inside of me, there's a treasure
That exceeds any measure!
Like the oyster, in fact,
I'm naturally prone to react
With a pearly layer of protection
To cover the cause of infliction.

My fruit of **peace** and **patience**
Can come to my rescue.
The handy gift of endurance
Can be an appeasing virtue
That gives strength and wisdom
And reflects God's Kingdom.

And what about **goodness,**
And the fruit of **kindness**?
At the time of any hard test,
My behavior can be at its best.
At this difficult testing hour
I can show my true color.
If I am truly God's child,
My thoughts won't go wild,

My life will be under the control
And the reign of Lord of all.

By His empowering grace,
I can cover any intense pain
With layers of heavenly peace,
I don't really need to complain.

If my pain turns into a jewel,
Then life won't seem so cruel.
In the end I can certainly win
If I can make a pearl within.

How Does the Cross Work?

*"Truly, I say to you, as you did it to one of the
least of these my brethren, you did it for me."*
(Matthew 25:40)

In the age of machinery, it is necessary to be able to work machines. Imagine your life without knowing how to operate a car, a computer, an answering machine, or a fax machine.

With the mentality of the age, a child went to his Sunday school teacher and said to her pointing at the cross hung on the wall, "Yesterday I was praying and I asked God to show me how to **operate the cross**."

With a broad grin, the teacher asked the boy, "Tell me, is there a button on the cross to activate it?"

The boy answered in amazement as if surprised how his teacher didn't understand how, "Of course not! It's very simple. I have the button in my heart. If I push it, I can open the door and allow Jesus to come in. Then He can **operate me**. Didn't He die on the cross to make me better?"

This little boy got it while we, grownups, struggle with the concept of Christianity. Often times, we like to work the cross or the Holy Spirit for ourselves. So, we use prayers as a button to push to be granted our heart's desire.

197

Actually, it is vice versa. The Holy Spirit works **through us** so we fulfill God's plan. When that happens, we reflect Christ on earth and people can see our light as Christians. Through the act of surrender and obedience through the will of God, He can guide us to live a glorious life that glorifies His name.

I Saw Jesus Before

I'm the product of divorce,
My parents fought a hard battle
And neither had any remorse
Thinking I was still too little.
They continued their fight,
And I wanted to hide.

When I couldn't take any more,
I used to leave 'n go next door
To our friendly neighbor
Who gave my life a different flavor.
I went to him with my fear,
Magically, he wiped every tear.
His kindness, I cannot forget
He taught me how to live hope
From morning to sunset,
He gave my life a new scope,

Then
I met my lovely wife to be.
She said, "I want you to meet
Someone Who's dear to me,
Someone Who's very sweet
He's the One Who set me free.
I want you to meet Him, too,
He is so faithful and true."

I saw His picture on the wall
And something struck my soul.
When I saw His radiant face,
Filled with heavenly grace,
I told her, I met Him before,
He was living next door."
She said, "But this is Jesus!"
I said, "He used to visit us
When I felt sad and alone
In our loveless home."
She asked, "Do you know
He used to live long time ago?"

I insisted, "I met Him before,
He was living next door.
He was our friendly neighbor
Who gave my life a different flavor.
His kindness I cannot forget,
He's the finest person I've met.

The Inward Condition of the Heart

"Woe to you, scribes and Pharisees, hypocrites!
For you are like whitewashed tombs, which
outwardly appear beautiful, but within they are
full of dead men's bones and all uncleanness."
(Matthew 23:27)

When you look at flowers in a clay pot, you forget about the plain pot and enjoy the beauty of the flowers. You unwrap a present, and no matter how beautiful the wrapping paper is, it ends up in the trashcan while you enjoy the gift.

You can use the most exquisite platter to serve your food. However, if the food is not palatable, it defeats the purpose. The real value lies, not in the container, but rather in the filling.

By the same token, you can beautify your apparel or your living conditions any way you want, but in God's eyes your toil is in vain without purifying your heart.

Often times we tend to beautify Christ's memory by wearing a cross or by honoring Him on Sundays and special occasions. However, this can merely be **outward,** yet the **inward condition of the heart** doesn't pledge allegiance to Jesus Christ.

"Looking good" is the plague of the age. This practice could lead to hypocrisy, dishonesty, conceit, and self-righteousness.

External religious conformity may look good, but it may be meaningless if the inner impurities are harbored.

On the other hand, if we pay attention to the materials used in the building of the tabernacle, we may find symbolism that represents the opposite picture to the former one. In building the **exterior** of the tabernacle, **bronze and silver** were the materials of choice for the posts and pegs, for example. However, **gold** was used in abundance in the making of furniture **inside** the tabernacle. One may get the impression that the inside of the tabernacle was much more important and more sacred than the outside, that's why God instructed that something real pure and precious, such as gold, be used on the inside.

The inside of the tabernacle was the residence of God, so it had to be appropriate for His holy presence. Now, in the New Testament, our hearts are supposed to be the temples of the Holy Spirit, so they have to be pure and well prepared for God's holy presence in our lives. Consequently, the **outer appearance of a Christian** can be humble as the bronze and silver in the exterior of the tabernacle. However, the **heart of a Christian** should be made out of gold as the interior of the tabernacle.

> *"Do you not know that your body is a temple of the Holy Spirit within you, which you have from God? You are not your own; you were bought with a price. So glorify God in your body."*
> (Corinthians 6:19, 20)

The Beauty Within

She saw beauty and glamour
Reflected on her fancy mirror.
She thought there was an error,
"That is not the right reflection!
With my dark side and affliction,
It should reflect imperfection.
With my sinful life and inequity,
With my carelessness and irresponsibility.
It shouldn't show me any magnanimity."

In her dejected state of mind
She didn't feel beautiful inside.
It was just a cover from outside.

A voice spoke to her gently
And directed her to the vanity.
She looked in that direction,
A box, grabbed her attention.
With precious stones, it was studded.
But the watch inside it, had rusted,
For years, it hasn't been running,
It was time for it to be replaced
With a newer watch, so stunning
Like the box in which it was placed.

In the watch, so old and useless,
She saw her heart, so restless.
It surely needed replacement
With a heart, pure 'n repentant.

The initial gentle voice
Started to be a cacophony
It was her conscience voice
That led to an epiphany.

Yes, in the mirror, she gazed
To see her reflected image.
A critical query was raised,
'N she got an important message.

In essence, beauty is like vapor,
As you grow old, it doesn't stay.
Beauty is like wrapping paper
The wrapper, you throw away,
Like the **gift**, that you keep 'n cherish,
Your good **soul**, will not ever perish.

Beauty will not be beauty
If it doesn't stem from within.
Beauty cannot be beauty
If the heart is full of sin.

"I" in Two Words

*"Has not God chosen those who are poor in
the world to be rich in faith and heirs of the
kingdom which He has promised to those who
love Him?"*

(James 2:5)

At a party, the guests were playing a game. Each one was
supposed to describe himself/herself in two words.

A man proudly said, "I'm a doctor and a golfer." A lady
said, "I'm a mother and a chauffer." Then it was Johnny's, a
six-year old boy's, turn. Without any hesitation, Johnny assured,
"I am Johnny Johnson."

For Johnny, it was very easy to identify himself as the son
of Mr. Johnson. Often times, children impress us with their
simple, yet profound answers. Johnny's answer came from the
realization that he belonged to a family and that was the heritage
that identified him.

We, as Christians, belong to the family of believers, the
church of God. Our Father is a Heavenly King, but do we really
identify ourselves as the children of God? **Do people see in
our life the characteristics of royalty? Do we honor our title
as heirs of God's Kingdom? Does God's light shine through**

our lives?

When the people of Israel had finished all the work in the tabernacle "as the Lord had commanded," **the glory of the Lord** filled the tabernacle. By the same token when we do God's work in humility and with utter obedience, God reveals Himself to us and His glory and radiance will be manifested to people through us. Only then can people recognize our royal heritage.

Royalty Shows on His Face

Swollen eyelids and puffy bags,
Aging spots and a double chin,
A facial skin that droops 'n sags,
But not concealing a sweet grin.

I gaped at his worn-out face
With wrinkles and aging signs,
But I could still see a trace
Of features that were so fine.

He was very sick and infirm
Though bed-ridden and tired,
His countenance did confirm
A serenity that I admired,
A complexion, so radiant,
And integrity, so salient,
An uplifted spirit, so confident,
And a status, so prominent.

"Are you a king's son?"
I asked with curiosity.
"To me you look like one
Who reflects royal majesty."

With vision, not so clear,
He asked me to draw near.

With a voice, so sincere,
He beckoned me to hear.
"Yes, I am a king's son
Not of this world, I claim.
He is Jesus Christ, the One
Whose mercy, I proclaim.
He rescued me from the pit,
He washed 'n cleansed my soul
I, the one who is not fit,
He chose to forgive 'n console.
That's why I chose to submit
My whole life to His control.
"When you are God's heir,
You're entitled to inherit
Characteristics, so fair.
It's not based on your merit,
It's pure grace, I should declare."